MORE FROM LIFE

S J CRABB

Copyrighted Material

Copyright © S J Crabb 2018

S J Crabb has asserted her rights under the Copyright, Designs and Patents Act 1988 to be identified as the Author of this work.

This book is a work of fiction and except in the case of historical fact, any resemblance to actual persons, living or dead, is purely coincidental. All rights reserved. No part of this book may be reproduced or transmitted in any form without written permission of the author, except by a reviewer who may quote brief passages for review purposes only.

NB: This book uses UK spelling.

ALSO BY S J CRABB

The Diary of Madison Brown
My Perfect Life at Cornish Cottage
My Christmas Boyfriend
Jetsetters
More from Life
A Special Kind of Advent
Fooling in love
Will You
Holly Island
Aunt Daisy's Letter
The Wedding at the Castle of Dreams
My Christmas Romance
Escape to Happy Ever After

sjcrabb.com

CHAPTER 1

Why does the phone always ring when you're in the middle of something? I've just raced upstairs to change for work and there it is. Ringing angrily downstairs commanding me to answer it, IMMEDIATELY. It won't be ignored and just about sums up my life. Always at the beck and call of everyone with no time for myself.

I try to ignore it as it's probably one of those call centres trying to sell me something I don't want or need. So, instead, I grab my uniform and do what I should have done twenty minutes ago – get ready for work.

Trying to block out the angry noise I kick the bedroom door shut. There! Successfully ignored.

Now I have major anxiety though. What if it was one of the kids, hurt or injured somewhere and calling for help? It may be the hospital informing me of the emergency unfolding right now. What if it's my mother? She may have been arrested in a foreign country for drug smuggling and needs me to organise bail and a crackpot

1

legal team. Mind you, the only crackpot in the drugs bust would be her.

The phone stops and I breathe a sigh of relief and set about the task in hand. Almost as soon as I have one foot in the polyester trouser leg it starts again.

Swearing like a trooper, I abandon what I'm doing and rush to the phone. Taking the stairs two at a time appears to be the norm these days as I race from one thing to another. *'Down Time'* is reserved for the perfect people. *'Me Time'* doesn't exist in my world and has no part in my life. Those luxuries are reserved for the yummy mummies who deposit their kids to the school in their Range Rover before heading to the gym for their daily workout with the hot personal trainer. Then afterwards they head to the spa for a body wrap followed by a healthy de-stressing lunch with their own kind.

Finally, I reach the phone and bark, "Yes."

Dead! Absolutely nothing, the line is silent and all I can hear are the screams in my mind. Typical. Angrily, I press 1471 to see who dared interrupt my day with their demanding ring. As I thought, the caller withheld their number. Bother, trust your instincts and listen to your head it never lets you down.

Well, almost - my head has a tendency to let me down in every decision I take. It's got to the point where I do the opposite of what it's telling me because whenever I listen to that little voice inside my head, it causes me no end of problems.

Like the time it told me to join the pre-mentioned gym. I went for it and kitted myself out in the sale at Primark and I thought I looked super cool and trendy. A fat lot of good it did me though. I only went on the running machine and proceeded to fall off that. I'm no great swimmer so even that was out of bounds and the most exercise I ever got was walking from the carpark and up the stairs to hell.

I even tried a Pilates class once until my own bodily functions let me down. Trust it to happen during the cool down period when there was maximum silence.

Pushing all irrelevant thoughts from my mind I concentrate on the job in hand. I'll be late for work unless I leave within the next five minutes.

Once again, I take the stairs two at a time and wrestle with the hated polyester trousers. I just have time to grab my fleece and slip on my practical ballerina pumps and I'm good to go.

So, in five minutes flat I've changed like wonder woman, secured the house and wheel spun out of the gravel drive.

Even though the drive only takes ten minutes, it feels like an hour as the time counts down to clock-in time. I couldn't speed if I wanted to because I'm driving my son's car which is fitted with a black box due to his age. 30 mph seems like 5 as the journey seems to last a lifetime.

I try not to breathe if at all possible because Ryan's car smells of old socks and stale body odour. I'm only allowed to use it because I promised him I'd fill it up with petrol on my way home. He doesn't need it until later, anyway. He's still at college and got a lift in with his friend Mungo – don't ask!

Finally, I drive into the car park and ignoring the far end, park as close to the doors as possible. We're supposed to leave them free for the customers but as I shop here, that would also be me.

I think I make it with two minutes to go and breathe a sigh of relief. Finally, my equivalent of downtime. I only do four hours but as far as I'm concerned, they are four hours where I can sit still on a chair and think of nothing. No phones are allowed and I take great delight in turning my buzzing nightmare from hell -off!

Susan the checkout supervisor smiles as I approach.

"Hi, Amanda. Bang on time as usual."

I grin. "Barely. One day I'll slip up but today is not that day."

She grins and winks mischievously. "I've put you on *baskets only* today. I'm sure you'll be happy with that position."

I shrug nonchalantly but inside I'm doing the happy-clappy dance and running a victory parade around my head.

"Sure, whatever."

She rolls her eyes as I saunter towards the prized position. Pure bliss. Four hours of gazing unashamedly at Veg man. Whoa, the coveted seat in the house is all mine today. Strange how something so innocent can totally make my day.

As I settle into my chair and sign into my register, I look around me. I have worked at Tescos for two years now and despite everything I love it. I get to escape from my daily life and sit for four hours, three times a week minus any overtime, in solitary bliss.

Here, I'm just a face and part of the furniture as I process the shopping and smile at the customers. Occasionally I share a joke or two with them and then they are gone. Nobody bothers me and I can totally switch off from what a nightmare my daily life is. Then there's the added bonus of gazing lustfully at Veg man.

He's the produce manager and likes nothing more than wielding his cucumbers and sorting his marrows. Although he is obviously younger than me it doesn't stop my mind from working overtime. He fills his manager's shirt with a body that looks as if he lives in the gym. I see the beginnings of a tattoo when he rolls up his sleeves and sigh inside. He looks like a male model and I imagine those capable hands wrapped around me as he declares his undying love for me.

I blame the HRT. Ever since I started on that wonder drug I've been out of control. No man is safe from my desperate gaze as I ogle every breathing man under 50 in the vicinity. I have so got to get a life and fast.

The first customer places their basket on the side and I smile happily. Time to switch off life and say hello to fantasy for the next four hours. How I love my job.

CHAPTER 2

It must be one hour in that he appears. As I look up, I see him hauling the potatoes into place. Luckily, I have no customers and can spy on him unashamedly from my seat in the front row. I watch his muscles ripple as he moves and sigh inside. I picture us a couple in a previous life and bet my life would have been so different with a man like him.

The reality is, I met and married the first man that asked me. Robert was in my class at college and we got together at a party one night. We became inseparable and dated for two years before he proposed after a Nando's one night.

I allowed my stupid head to interfere again and persuade me he was the one. My heart, though, was telling me otherwise. Robert was my first boyfriend and as it turned out also my last. We were good friends, and I enjoyed his company but there was never that spark between us. It seemed the inevitable step to take and so I accepted his proposal because I didn't want to upset him. You see, that's me, always wanting to please everyone over and above my own needs. Some may say it's an admirable quality, others would call me a doormat.

It's no wonder things never worked out. We had two children Ryan and Saskia and then just before I started at Tescos he left me for a woman in his re-enactment circle. They bonded over a fake battle and have been inseparable ever since.

To be honest, it was a relief. Finally, I got to sleep without listening to a snoring concerto every night. The remote control was now my exclusive property as the kids have TVs in their rooms and rarely venture out from them. The toilet seat is largely clean and firmly shut and my satin monogrammed towels remain folded neatly in place in the bathroom. Well, that's all the time the kids are out, anyway.

Another customer interrupts my trip down memory lane and grins.

"Hey, Mandy, how's life treating you?"

I stifle the irritation as I see my neighbour Eddie Barker.

"Fine thanks, Eddie, how's Maureen? Has she recovered from the dog bite yet?"

Eddie rolls his eyes. "Usual drama queen. The poor puppy didn't even scratch the skin. Typical Maureen though, straight down the doctors for a tetanus. I told her we shouldn't get a dog but she couldn't stop watching those programmes on rescue dogs. It was always going to end in tears – mainly mine."

Laughing, I start scanning his shopping.

As he packs it away he says with concern, "I saw your car's out of action again. Can I help out with anything?"

Shaking my head, I pull a face. "It's fine. I've called the AA out for a home start tomorrow. They couldn't do today so I was reduced to taking Ryan's car."

He looks at me sympathetically. "Bad luck."

I grin as he says softly.

"You know, I could always take a look at it for you. I used to be a mechanic and I'm sure it's nothing much."

I smile to myself. Eddie used to mend hoovers in Currys. Hardly what I'd call a mechanic. But his heart's in the right place and I almost forgive him for moving in next door. Then I remember the loud television as he invited half the street in to watch the boxing, football or any other sport for that matter. Then there are the loud parties and the screaming arguments. No, Maureen and Eddie are not Margo and Jerry from the Good Life, more like the neighbours from hell.

I smile brightly. "Oh, thanks but it's fine. It's all arranged and I'm sure it's nothing. You know me, I don't know anything about how mechanical things work. Maybe I'll do a course at evening classes."

I stifle a giggle as Eddie looks horrified.

"You don't wanna be doing that, Mandy. The people that do those classes aren't like us you know."

In my mind, I've enrolled already!

By the time Eddie leaves, I look up and Veg man has gone. Typical, now I'll have to wait for him to re-stock his trolley before I can lust after him once more.

Four hours pass in a flash and after only one more sighting of Veg man, I start the short trip home via the petrol station.

As usual, I am conned into filling Ryan's car to the brim whereas he just puts in five pounds worth and then asks me to lend him more.

It's not as if I've got money to spare. When Robert left, I got the house and nothing else. Money's tight and my hours at Tescos helps with the bills and food with not a lot left over for anything else. I receive some benefits and whatever Robert decides to spare each month but things are difficult.

I watch as a black Range Rover squeals into place beside me. A stick-thin woman jumps out wearing those oversized designer sunglasses. Her hair is neatly pulled back in a ponytail and she's wearing jodhpurs that accentuate every curve of a supermodel's body. She is immaculate and fills her space with the usual air of boredom that the perfect people adopt in public. This is obviously such an inconvenience. She probably longs for the days when a little attendant would rush forward and fill your car for you without you even having to exit the vehicle. She must spend about £100 on fuel and not even register the cost. We are both women of roughly the same age but it's obvious our lives are totally different.

My heart sinks as I contemplate my life. Where did it all go so wrong?

CHAPTER 3

I think I make it home with half an hour to spare. I just have time to change out of my uniform and into my 'lounging clothes' or to everyone else my tracksuit from Primark. As I hear the key in the door, I wonder what it will be today.

As the door opens the usual hell breaks loose. Saskia enters like the complete drama queen she is and dramatically drops her bag to the floor. Kicking it to the side she whines, "Sophie Edwards is a complete bitch."

I sigh inside. Instead, I smile like the good mother I am.

"Hi, darling. How was your day?"

"Just take a look at this Instagram picture. What was she thinking wearing that skirt with that top? Social suicide and I can't think why she has a boyfriend and I don't."

She flashes the phone at me but it looks a blur.

"You know, she thinks she's so cool with her *'Vlog'* I mean, who wants fashion tips from someone who wears orange on a weekly basis. Total loser and it's not even as if she has that many subscribers."

She makes towards the stairs and I say half-heartedly, "Would you like a drink?"

All I get is the sound of the door slamming shut behind her.

Oh well, today is a good day. I prefer the angry girl to the emotional one any day.

Before I can even grab her lunch box from her school/handbag the door opens and Ryan slouches in.

He also throws his bag to the floor and just nods as he moves past me and heads into the kitchen.

Once again, I tidy his bag and collect his lunch box and follow him inside.

"Hi, darling. How was your day?"

Nothing, not even the usual grunt. Maybe he didn't hear me. I mean, his head's so far inside the fridge he may not make it out alive.

He grabs some pork pies and scotch eggs and heads towards the door without so much as a word. Desperately, I say in a rather high voice, "Um, thanks for the car. I filled it with petrol."

He doesn't look back and just grunts as he heads outside the room.

Well, that's that then. The teenagers from hell are home and now safely ensconced in their pits for the evening. I won't see either of them until dinner and I sigh again.

I actually think my children hate me. The looks they shoot me say it all. I'm a dinosaur - old - with nothing worth saying. I don't understand and they can't be bothered to explain.

As I clear up, I think about the two gorgeous children I raised. Two beautiful children who thought I was everything and to them I was. I could do no wrong and they craved my attention. We used to enjoy days out and making things with boxes and glue. We spent endless hours having fun, and I never thought for one minute what lie ahead.

It's like a little piece of loveliness fell away with every inch they gained. All that's left is the lonely life of a single parent with two teenagers from hell.

I am interrupted from my despondent thoughts by the phone ringing. Once again, I flash it an irritable glance. Not another call centre - please!

Luckily, it's no such thing and I'm happy to hear the excited tones of my best friend Tina. I say Tina but she was actually christened Titiana Cunningham. Apparently, the registrar got distracted by her mother's rather enormous breasts at the registration of her birth. He substituted Tatiana for Titiana, thereby subjecting her to a lifetime of bullying and verbal abuse. She shortened it to Tina, but the damage had already been done. I think we bonded over our devastating names. Mine wasn't nearly so bad but Amanda Swallows is hardly the stuff of dreams. I was glad to get married and ditch it but Dickin wasn't much better.

Tina sounds happy and I smile as she says excitedly, "Hey, Amanda, do you fancy catching up at the Spotted Dog later? I've got so much to tell you."

Although she can't see me, I nod enthusiastically.

"Great, what time?"

"Make it 7. I'll meet you in the resident's bar."

"Ok, see you later."

I hang up feeling in a better mood. Tina's such good fun and we haven't caught up in ages. She's a little crazy but I love her to bits. I don't know what I would have done without her when Robert left. You certainly need your friends at times like those and she stood up and was very much counted.

I start to get the dinner ready, happy to have some plans at least. I can't remember the last time I went out for the evening and feel excited at being let loose on the town for the night.

By the time the kids from hell join me for dinner, I couldn't care less about their moods. I dish up the Spaghetti Bolognese and ignore their raised eyes.

Saskia groans. "Can't you make anything else occasionally? I'm going to look like a piece of spaghetti at this rate."

Ryan nods. "It's getting kind of old. Mungo's mum makes a mean curry and they have all sorts of exotic food."

Saskia shudders. "You can keep that spicy food away from me. I want healthy things; my spots are off the scale at the moment and I need to feed my skin."

I laugh softly. "Well, maybe you should ease off the chocolate for five minutes and they may clear up."

Ryan laughs as Saskia screeches. "Are you seriously blaming me for my hormonal breakouts? I mean, are you? Really?"

I shake my head and try to ignore her. Maybe she'll calm down if I don't react.

No, she doesn't.

"I mean, it's not as if I haven't tried every product on the market that promises the world and never delivers. How am I supposed to get a boyfriend looking like zitzilla?"

Ryan laughs out loud and I throw him a warning glare. Saskia shouts, "It's ok for you, douche bag. Guys have it so easy. All they have to do is show an interest and the girls come running. Mind you, I pity the poor girl who grabs your attention. I mean, you're hardly Justin Bieber, are you?"

Ryan just laughs even harder and takes a picture on his phone of his ranting sister. This act alone makes her explode.

"Delete that you, idiot. If I see one photo of me on your social media, then I'm getting my revenge. God, why couldn't you give me a sister? My life sucks living in this hell hole. Chloe Smith doesn't have to put up with this abuse. She has a sister who helps her with her homework and does her skincare regime for her. Do us all a favour and go and live with dad and his corpse bride."

I know I should chastise her about her reference to the corpse bride but I get a sadistic kick out of hearing it. Despite the fact it was an amicable conscious uncoupling I still feel hurt that he found someone to replace me before I even knew I was being replaced.

Lucy Williams actually does look like the corpse bride. She's a little gothic and wears black at all times. Her hair is long and black and her makeup heavy and um… well, black, actually. She has very pale skin and bright red lips like Morticia. The total opposite of me but she seems nice enough. I mean, she's always been pleasant when I've seen her at the odd family function, like Uncle Bert's funeral. I remember thinking how at home she looked among the gargoyles on the church pews.

She must have something though because Robert isn't the sort to fall head over heels for just any old woman – I should know, he married me after all.

Saskia pushes back her seat angrily and shouts, "I'll be in my room under a face pack. God only knows I have to do something proactive to combat the onslaught of maturity."

As she heads off, I say loudly, "Oh, I'm heading out to meet Tina later."

She turns around and shoots me an incredulous look.

"What, you're going out – tonight?"

Ryan also looks put out and I shake my head. "Why, is that a problem?"

Saskia snarls. "God, you're so selfish. What sort of mother deserts her children for the pub in their moment of crisis? Remind me of the number for ChildLine, will you?"

I start to laugh which only adds fuel to the raging fire. She shouts,

"Look at you, you don't even realise how selfish you are. Chloe Smith's mum never goes out. She's always there with a motherly shoulder to lean on when the going gets tough. She's not out drinking with the old folks pretending to be young again. God, you're so embarrassing."

She storms off and I look at Ryan for some moral support, He just follows her and grunts. "I'll be on my Xbox. I'm going out with Mungo later, remember."

Sighing, I start to clear the dishes. It's at times like this that I wish I had someone here to provide back up. A man who loves me and puts me before everyone else. Someone to hold me and tell me everything's going to be ok. Someone to chase away the harsh realities of life and kiss it all better.

As Veg man's face swims into view, I picture him kissing me better and feel instantly – well, better actually. At least we have our fantasies to sustain us through the most testing times.

CHAPTER 4

Despite my children, I change out of my loungewear and into my pub wear. Black knee length dress with killer heels and pashmina. Standard issue for any middle-aged woman out on the town and trying to blend in.

Luckily, I can walk to the pub which saves me from begging a lift from my son. It's quite a nice evening and I take a moment to enjoy the fact I'm out on the town for once. Usually, I spend the evening ironing in front of Emmerdale followed by whatever rubbish is on. This will make a welcome change.

I feel a little nervous as I push my way through the door to the Resident's bar. Maybe it's my age but I don't feel comfortable walking into a bar on my own. However, I'm greeted almost immediately by a loud, "Amanda, over here."

Looking in the direction of the voice, I relax as I see my friend Tina. She waves me over and smiles happily as I sit down.

"I've got you a drink. Double vodka and coke just like in our youth."

Giggling, I unwrap myself from my pashmina and grab the drink gratefully.

"I so need this. The kids from hell were particularly hellish this evening and Saskia has major acne. Well, you can imagine the atmosphere at home."

Tina laughs. "Tell me about it. Sutton is into some new YouTube channel and spends all evening with her headphones on. I talk to myself most of the time. And as for Croydon, well, he is permanently glued to his noise reduction headphones and lives in a virtual world for most of the day, only re-surfacing to planet Earth when his stomach dictates it."

Shaking my head, I picture Tina's crazy family. She's married to Derek, a totally gorgeous man who idolises her. He works as a dentist which keeps him very busy and enables Tina to live her life like a perfect person. Their children were named after the places they used to date which is a little unconventional but somehow doesn't seem that strange anymore.

I can tell that Tina is excited about something and look at her with interest.

"Go on, tell me your news."

She laughs happily and fidgets on her seat.

"I can't hide anything from you, can I, darling?"

Shaking my head, I take another sip of the calming liquid.

"Well, you know how Derek's been promising to take a break for absolutely ages."

I nod as she squeals, "He's only gone and booked us a luxury suite on the Island of Antigua for a romantic break without the children."

I smile happily. "That's fantastic. You deserve this so

much, what's it been, three years since you had a holiday?"

She nods emphatically. "Yes, unless you count our annual Easter break at Centre Parcs with the kids."

"So, what about them? Do you want me to look out for them?"

Tina shakes her head looking very pleased with herself.

"No need, granny's invited them to her Villa in Spain for the duration. They get a holiday too and so we're all happy. I must say, it's been a long time coming and now it's actually happening. We leave in two weeks' time and it can't come soon enough for me."

Despite feeling completely and utterly jealous of my friend, I'm happy for her. She doesn't see a lot of Derek and manages to fill her time by working in several local charity shops and filling in at the local school when they need volunteers. Despite the fact they aren't short of money they are short on time - well Derek is, anyway.

So, for the next two hours and twenty minutes I let her talk about the single most exciting thing that has happened to her in years and try not to listen to the part of me that wishes it was me.

By the time I get home, my ears are ringing. Tina can certainly chat and all I could do was nod and keep downing the double vodkas. I feel quite light-headed now and just want a nice hot bath and bed.

Ryan's car is gone and I feel the flutter of anxiety in my stomach again. I know he's 18 now, but he will always be my little boy. Is it wrong of me to pray that he failed his driving test? All the time he was a learner I had to sit next to him. Now he could be anywhere and I can never fully relax until he's home where he belongs.

The house greets me like a stranger would. It feels empty and cold and there are no warm lights to welcome me in and the heating has gone off leaving a chill in the air. It feels empty and where it was once filled with family activity, now it's just a place to keep my things and my children, of course.

They don't want my company though and who can blame them? I know nothing about Snapchat, or whatever else they use to communicate these days. My limit is Facebook and I only use this to stalk people. It's amazing what you can find out if you delve deep enough. I know I shouldn't but I regularly surf Robert and Lucy's pages, looking for any sign of unhappiness or the strain beginning to show. Not yet though. There are just happy snaps of them looking like loved-up teenagers as they share the life Robert tried to make me involved with.

As hard as I tried I never really took to re-enactment battles and watching endless documentaries on war and the like. I was happier watching Keeping up with the Kardashians with Saskia and Modern Family.

It came back to bite me though when Robert informed me he had met someone else and was leaving me.

The saddest thing of all was I was happy for him. Once again, the doormat surfaced and I remember hugging him goodbye and wishing him every happiness. What an idiot? Who does that?

I suppose it just showed we weren't right for each other after all. The only thing I could think of was that I would have the house to myself and not have him moaning at me all the time about lunch and dinner and what was in his sandwiches that day. I could watch box sets of trash TV and not feel his judgemental stare. I could dance naked in the bedroom without fear of him pouncing on me for some dutiful marital sex. I gave up wearing sexy nightwear years ago in case I drew his amorous attentions. All I wanted my bed for was to sleep.

Now he's gone it's all I can think of. I stare at hunky men in the street and wonder what it would be like to have sex with them. I find myself wiggling down the aisles at work hoping to draw a hot guy's attention. I blame the hot flushes and the HRT. Something's happening to me and it's such a waste I'm single. By the time I find a man the urge will have gone and I'll be firmly planted in knitting circles and away days to Bognor Regis with Epsom Coaches.

The light snaps on momentarily blinding me and I take in the scary sight of bedtime teenager.

Saskia stands at the top of the stairs with her arms folded and her hair in a towel and some crazy green stuff on her face. She taps her foot angrily and shouts, "We ran out of chocolate and there are no Kettle crisps. You left me home alone with no food and anybody could have come in and stolen me."

Fighting back the manic laughter threatening to explode at the thought of anyone willingly kidnapping the monster before me, I just look contrite.

"I'm sorry, I thought the bowl of fruit and healthy nutbars would make a nutritious snack. I forgot you're allergic to vitamins and minerals."

She rolls her eyes and shakes her head at the moron who gave birth to her.

"Ryan left ages ago and I'm bored."

She looks at me accusingly and I shake my head. "What do you want to do then?"

She heads towards me and looks fairly animated for once. "You grab the popcorn and I'll stick on an episode of embarrassing bodies. God knows I need something to distract me from my own body's betrayal."

Sighing, I head into the kitchen to do as I'm told. So much for bath and bed. The guilt is preventing me from telling her no. I always thought I'd be that stern but fair mother who raised her children with a no-nonsense attitude and took no prisoners.

Well, life got in the way and I soon reverted to the trap we all fall into – *anything for an easy life*. Well, once again my head got it wrong. All it did was make it an impossible future. If I'd been stronger at the beginning instead of the harassed mother of two floundering around wishing the kids had arrived with a manual, maybe I would have my dream children now. I only have myself to blame and accept my punishment with as much good grace as I can.

They'll grow out of it – won't they?

CHAPTER 5

As mornings go mine are always fairly easy. The kids surface after many trips upstairs to wake them, usually 15 minutes before they have to leave. Saskia gets the school bus and Ryan drives to College. Or at least I think he does.

He goes somewhere even though he has several free periods. I did think of installing a tracking device in his car but being electronically challenged, I soon gave up on that idea.

I know I could track their phones but they are way cleverer than me and would probably block me or something. Not that I have the faintest idea how to do it, anyway. I only know about it because they have obviously tracked mine. Unbeknown to me they set it up and I'm always getting texts like *'While you're in Boots can you pick up some sanitary towels?'* or *"Grab me some antifreeze from the petrol station."*

At first, it really spooked me. It was as if they were watching my every move and it was only when I mentioned it to my mum that she explained how it all worked. My mum's been a social media queen since it was invented. Nothing gets past her and she has 1500 Facebook friends and 2000 twitter followers. She runs several Facebook groups and her Instagram is amazing.

She knows absolutely everything about everybody and is a virtual encyclopaedia of gossip and knowledge of just about the whole population of Surrey.

She's a force to be reckoned with and the hellish teenagers absolutely adore her.

My thoughts are interrupted by the doorbell ringing. Finally, the man from the AA.

I'm actually feeling really excited. A man in a uniform does that to me. I hope he's gorgeous. I've been fantasising about a strong capable man tending to my engine for weeks now. It was after Alison from the bakery section told me about the hot mechanic who saved her from a breakdown on a country road one night. As luck would have it my car broke down just in time for me to hopefully live out a similar fantasy.

So, with a deep breath and setting my features into sex siren mode I fling open the door and just stare.

Surely there must be some mistake?

I look around but no, the woman standing in front of me wearing the orange jacket of the fourth emergency service looks at me kindly.

"You need a home start I believe."

I look at her in surprise and she laughs softly.

"Surprised you, have I? Well, don't worry it happens all the time."

The disappointment creeps over me like moss on a stone and changes my mood instantly. I nod and try to get a grip of my manners.

"Yes, sorry. I mean, I wouldn't usually call someone out but I had no way of getting it to the garage."

She nods towards the car.

"Grab your keys and I'll take a look."

I do as she asks and follow her sorrowfully to the car. Just my luck. Probably the only woman in the world who chose this as a career option has shattered my fantasy in a heartbeat. Just typical.

I hand her the keys and watch as she diagnoses the problem. Despite my disappointment, I've got to admire her. She seems to know what she's doing and I feel ashamed of myself for wishing she was male. I mean, surely, I should applaud the fact that this woman is as good as any man. The trouble is, it wasn't her mechanical skills that interested me. I am now officially out of control. Any opportunity at all to ogle a poor unsuspecting man just to stoke my lady fire fantasies.

I really should consult the doctor about HRT aversion therapy. This is making me ill.

Pauline, my new best mechanical friend is a marvel. In no time the broken beast is roaring into life again and she didn't even break a fingernail. Respect to Pauline, she's amazing.

"There you go, just your battery. I've given it a charge but you should get to the nearest garage for a new one. They'll fit it for you and then you shouldn't have any more problems."

Smiling, I remember my manners.

"Thanks, Pauline. You know, it must be a great job for a woman. All those hunky men surrounding you every day. I wish I'd thought of it."

The look she throws me reminds me I'm bordering on insanity and shrugs. "It's ok. I don't see them though. I like it that way. Just me and the open road fixing people's problems and hopefully making them have a better day."

I nod towards the house.

"Do you fancy a cup of tea as a reward for all your hard work?"

She shakes her head and consults her clipboard.

"No, thanks, I've another job to go to. Good luck with the car, Amanda and I hope Veg man notices you today."

Feeling myself colour up, I remember that I've poured out my life story in ten minutes flat to a complete stranger. What must she think of me?

I've always been the same. Within minutes of meeting someone, I divulge every bit of information about my life before I even know their name. I really should join a friendship group somewhere. Preferably one full of hot men and women who look like King Kong to give me a better chance with the men.

Oh well, there's always Veg man like she said and I really should get off to work.

CHAPTER 6

It must be a week later that my mum returns from her cruise around the Balearics. As soon as I open the door, I'm greeted by the overpowering scent she always wears and am enveloped in a huge mummy hug. She shrieks, "Amanda, darling. Let me look at my baby."

Pulling back, she casts her critical gaze over me and smiles.

"Hm, you could do with a good meal inside you and a shopping trip to Zara. I see you've been pounding a trail to Primark again young lady. You know I've always told you to invest in some good quality items and mix and match. This cheap stuff from China or wherever it hails from will only take one wash before it loses it shape."

She pushes past me and looks around the house critically.

"You know, I always forget how small this house is. But then again, I'm used to bigger things now that I've found my sea legs. The cabins on the Anastasia were as big as the whole of the downstairs of this house. You really should come with me my dear and I'll fix you up with a hot sailor or a wealthy businessman."

Now I'm interested. My mother's always been a wise woman and suddenly I'm happy for her to take charge.

I nod enthusiastically. "That sounds great. Do you really think I could come with you?"

She laughs. "I'm only joking with you. Of course, a cruise is no place for a mother of two who thinks a good night out is watching Saturday Night takeaway. You should mingle darling and join some classes or clubs. I think there's a new country club opening up soon, maybe you should join."

My heart sinks. As if, the gym was bad enough and where would I get the money for a country club? I think my mother forgets that I live on the breadline.

I set about making her a cup of tea and we hear the front door crash open. My heart flips as I wonder what mood will be coming through it today.

My mum heads out and I hear shrieks and giggles as she greets the teenagers from hell. Even Ryan breaks out in a smile as they follow her into the kitchen excitedly.

Mum is in her element and beams around at us. "Saskia, look at you. You must have grown three inches since I saw you last month and that acne is definitely going down, you beautiful supermodel you."

Saskia preens herself and flicks her hair. "Oh, you noticed. Yes, it was that cream you recommended. It obviously suits my skin and has been a marvel. Much better than the Nivea mum always swears by."

She throws me a condescending look as my mum laughs.

"Yes, things have moved on since your mother was young. It's all in Cosmo, darling. You should never have cancelled your subscription you know. It's no wonder you're behind the times."

She turns to Ryan. "Darling, you look good enough to eat. I expect the hearts are leaving a shattered trail behind you, young man."

He just grins and I look at him in shock. Wow, his face really changes when he smiles. With a pang, I realise I haven't seen him smile much lately which is why it's surprised me now. I wonder if he's happy.

Mum carries on chatting as I fret about my children. Are they happy? I know children suffer as the result of a divorce. I thought they were cool with it but maybe they have been psychologically damaged forever and I was too wrapped up in my own loneliness to notice.

I watch as they all look at something on my mum's phone and laugh fit to burst. I feel very out of the loop and wish that I had the same relationship with them that my mum obviously does. At some point in all of this we fell into the routine of them living in their rooms and me existing downstairs like a servant in Downton Abbey.

I shake myself out of it as I hear Robert's name mentioned.

"So, are you part of the wedding party?"

Saskia groans. "Unfortunately, yes. I'm a bridesmaid and Ryan's an usher. We tried everything to get out of it but Dad won't budge."

I listen with interest. I don't know anything at all about my ex-husbands impending nuptials and haven't liked to show an interest in case they think I'm pining for him still.

Ryan groans. "I wish it was over already. I hate wearing a suit and it makes me look like an undertaker."

Of course, black will feature heavily in this wedding, it goes without saying.

Saskia laughs. "Oh Gran, you should see my dress. It's bright red to signify the blood of the fallen. Lucy's words, not mine."

My mum looks at me incredulously and says loudly, "Why would they want that?"

Saskia rolls her eyes. "Something to do with their re-enactment friends. Apparently, they wanted to get married in France among the war graves. The reception is to be a mass barbeque followed by a recreation of the battle of the Somme. I mean, please, who are these people? Ryan and I have decided as soon as they are changing we're out of there back to the hotel for a drink in the bar followed by a leisurely spa. I mean, who wants that for their wedding?"

My mum looks shocked. "Good god, it's utter madness. Are you sure you'll be safe among gun wielding nutters?"

We all laugh and I take some satisfaction in picturing the scene. My mum wipes the tears from her eyes and splutters, "When is the happy day?"

Ryan groans. "Next week. We head off on Friday and the wedding's on Saturday. The trouble is, we're booked in for the week and have to endure organised activities for the rest of it."

Saskia looks at me accusingly. "Honestly mum you really should put your foot down. Tell dad we can only stay for two days and you need us back. I'm not joking this is tantamount to child abuse."

My mum laughs as I shrug my shoulders.

"Sorry darling, you know the rules. Holidays are his. It's half term and you have to spend the week with him. It's in the settlement and I could get arrested if I disobeyed a court order."

I have to turn away before she sees the relief in my

eyes. I actually can't wait for a bit of peace and quiet for a week. Blissful solitude and several M&S meals for one, heading my way.

Once dinner is out of the way, the kids disappear back to their lairs and I settle down for a catch-up with my mother.

It's nice to have someone to talk to for once and it's at times like these that I realise how lonely I really am.

She looks at me with her razor-sharp stare and says with concern, "You look tired, Amanda. How are you coping?"

I shrug. "Mostly fine, I think."

She shakes her head. "How do you feel about Robert's wedding? It must hurt thinking of it."

I try to put on a brave face but she is my mother after all and the tears well up in my eyes.

"It's hard, mum. I'm not saying I wish we were still together, even I realised it was always going to happen. We were never really that couple who live in each other's pockets and finish each other's sentences. We were always more like best friends and the passion died in our relationship a long time ago, if it was ever really there in the first place."

Mum looks even more concerned. "That's terrible, darling. You mean, you've never experienced that Mills & Boon romance where your heart races and you lose your mind whenever he is near?"

Thinking of Veg man I know where she's coming from. I have that with him – in my fantasies only though.

"No, never. Although I know what you mean. It's just harder to find the one to make it happen."

Mum hands me a Ferrero Rocher and looks thoughtful.

"Maybe you do need a holiday. You're too old for

those 18-30 ones where they attend foam parties and sleep with the entire hotel in a mass orgy, but there are other ways."

I look at her in horror, "That's disgusting. Do they really do that?"

She laughs and nods vigorously. "Yes. When we were on a cruise, we stopped there one night. Well, I certainly learned a thing or two. It took me back to my fortnight on the Kibbutz last year."

Leaning forward, I look at her with interest. "Why, what happened there?"

Lowering her voice, she says excitedly. "Well, I didn't know what to expect but when I arrived I soon discovered the theme was very much sharing- and I mean, everything."

I look at her in shock and she grins. "Yes, exactly. It was certainly an eye opener and even I was shocked. I only went because it was on my bucket list and the things I saw there will haunt me to my dying day. It was like nothing I've ever seen before. It was so shocking I could only stand it for two weeks before I had to come home."

She winks as I look at her incredulously. "Two weeks! Mother, you're not saying..."

Laughing, she reaches for the chocolates. "Even I have my limits, darling. But we're talking about you. I think a holiday is just what you need."

I stare at her and feel my heart sinking. "I wish. The most I can afford is to pay for a trip to the cinema to watch Mamma Mia or something along those lines. Now it's just me I have to watch the pennies because the pounds are in short supply."

Mum settles back in her chair.

"Where there's a will there's a way. I'll have a think

about it and come up with something. You can find anything on the Internet these days and I'll send out a tweet to see if my network has any ideas."

My heart sinks as I realise my impending holiday is as fanciful an idea as that my mother will ever grow up. Fixing a smile on my face, I jump up to fetch us another cup of tea and those cookies I was saving for special occasions. No, this is my life now. Dreams are for the young and wishful thinking for the elderly. I deal in reality and it bites hard.

As I head off, I turn back and say sadly, "You know, mum. I don't know what happened, really. When I was younger, I thought I had it all. My life stretched before me and seemed full of exciting possibilities. I suppose I was so busy doing what I thought I should I lost sight of what was out there. Don't you ever look back and wish you'd done things differently?"

She looks at me in surprise and shakes her head. "No, I don't. I'm happy with all the choices I made and still am today. I wouldn't change a thing and have zero regrets."

I smile and say in a small voice. "I'm glad mum, really I am. Now let me get that tea."

As I head into the kitchen, I push down the huge wave of sadness that threatens to drag me under and the little voice in my heart speaks up for once as the realisation hits me hard – I want more from life, I suppose I always have.

CHAPTER 7

I can't believe my eyes. I've turned up to work and Veg man is wearing a suit. Wow! He looks super-hot and yet cool at the same time. He must have a manager's meeting or something. I suppose it's tough at the top and being a manager isn't all about juggling sprouts and arranging cauliflowers. My imagination is now suffering a near meltdown as I picture our future together.

I just need to get him to notice me and then future here I come.

I almost glide to my checkout wrapped in a haze of lust, love and even more lust.

Unfortunately, my checkout faces the freezer section today. Just my luck when he's looking super-hot and all.

Susan the checkout manager pops by after half an hour and smiles.

"How are you, honey? It feels like ages since I saw you."

Shrugging, I toss my hair like a supermodel in the hope Veg man is watching me.

"Oh, you know, same old."

She laughs. "How about we catch up over a coffee at lunch? There's something I want to run by you."

I smile with surprise as she moves quickly away before I can ask her what about. This is interesting. I know I hold the record of scanning the most items in a five-minute time period but other than that, I'm not sure what it could be about.

I spend the next hour worrying about it. Maybe they are getting rid of staff and I'm the first person on the list. Maybe they are swapping people around and… oh my god… I could end up in produce. Suddenly, I'm excited. This is it, I just know it. Our eyes will meet over a potato trolley and he will immediately fall in love with me. I really think this could happen. I've pictured it in my mind several times so it's surely now a reality.

The time drags until Susan stops by and pulls the little gate across signifying the closure of the checkout. Freedom and future beckon.

We head towards the staff canteen and the curiosity is burning me up inside.

I'm not sure what we even talk about on the way because my imagination is now officially out of control.

We grab a subsidised lunch of salad and a cold drink and take our seats near the window with the best view of the car park. It feels good to be free of the checkout for a while and I look towards the woman who holds my future in her hand expectantly.

She smiles softly. "How are you, Amanda? We rarely get any chance to talk these days, life is so hectic, isn't it?"

Smiling, I just hope I'm not showcasing a mouthful of lettuce as I nod. "It's fine. I struggle on but the kids are at a difficult stage and I'm not even sure I recognise them anymore."

She laughs. "We've all been there. Teenagers are a species all of their own. We spend most of the time disapproving of everything they do and comparing it to our own good old days. It doesn't take long to fall into the traps of our parents and start saying things like, *'We never did that in our day. By your age I was already... and the music today is nowhere near as good as in my youth.'* You get the picture."

Laughing, I have to agree. "Things have changed so much since I was young and we didn't have all this technology to worry about. I was just thrown out of the door with my bike and not expected back until lunchtime. There was no TV to glue me to the settee and no phone to replace speaking with my actual friends face to face. These days all they do is sit in their bedrooms and speak virtually. I'm not sure it's healthy, really. I mean, Ryan spends most of his time on his Xbox saving the world or causing its destruction and the only time I see him is when we have a power cut or he wants food. Saskia is following every celebrity blogger or should I say *Vlogger* and repeating their observations as if it's gospel. I'm then dispatched to buy the newest wonder product that will completely change her life while she looks for the next one. Her greatest ambition in life is to own a PO Box like Zoella and have freebies delivered there by the truckload every day. What happened to working at a bank as a career option? Mind you, even they've gone automated so there's no hope for any of them, really."

Susan laughs and nods in agreement and then turns to me and delivers her big secret.

"You know, that brings me to the reason I invited you to lunch."

I lean forward, the curiosity now burning a hole deep inside me bigger than any bout of indigestion.

She clears her throat and suddenly looks all business-like.

"We – as in the management here - are always on the lookout for workers who excel at what they do and may progress within the organisation."

I look at her with fascination. Whoa, she's suddenly switched to manager mode and looks very impressive.

She carries on. "Now your children are older we were thinking you may have more time on your hands. We were wondering if you may consider joining our management trainee programme. You would spend time in each of our departments and we'll train you in every aspect of management and what it involves. Of course, it's a full-time position, so the pay is considerably more than what you're on at the moment."

She leans back and looks at me triumphantly. "So, what do you say, can I sign you up?"

My mind buzzes with everything she's said. This is all quite unexpected and I never really thought about it before. But now I am it's looking quite an attractive proposition. I wonder if I could start in produce – this afternoon?

I can feel her scrutiny as she looks at me for my reaction and smile happily.

"Thank you, Susan, I really appreciate the offer. Can I talk it through with my children and give you my answer tomorrow?"

She smiles. "Of course, think it over and let me know. From my own experience it's the best thing I ever did.

It's really opened up a whole new world of possibilities and was the best decision I ever made."

Before I can reply I watch her face soften and look at someone approaching. As I turn around I almost choke on my drink because none other than Veg man is standing behind me looking like he needs me to jump on him immediately. Goodness, up close he's even more gorgeous and I feel flustered and totally out of my mind with desire.

He grins. "Sorry to interrupt ladies but I've just put a whole load of reduced tomatoes on the shelves in the staff shop. Make sure you grab them before they go."

As he turns to leave, I sit on my hands to stop me from grabbing something else before it goes and watch his retreating figure approach the next table with a sigh. The thought of gazing at him at the weekly manager's meeting makes my decision for me. This is a done deal. I'm so going to say yes and pull on the shirt of management responsibility. This is definitely meant to be.

Turning back to Susan, she nods towards Veg man. "Impressive, isn't he?"

Shaking my head, I say matter-of-factly, "Oh, I suppose so. A bit young for me though."

She sighs and nods in agreement. "Tell me about it. Some girls have all the luck. In his case it's Emily Symons from Florence and Fred. They've been dating for months now and she must be now considered one of the luckiest women alive."

WHAT!! My good mood evaporates instantly and my world ends. Veg man has a girlfriend, and she works here!!!

Suddenly, life has no meaning anymore and my earlier excitement has turned to dust. This doesn't happen in Mills & Boon. The heroine doesn't find out the hero has another girlfriend or is married already. This isn't right, surely?

Susan smiles and looks business-like once more as she consults her watch.

"Oh well, time is the enemy again. Let me know your decision tomorrow, Amanda and I'll set the ball rolling if you agree."

Nodding miserably, I follow her out.

CHAPTER 8

I return home and wait for the impending mood swing to crash through the door. I'm hoping for some sort of normal today because if anyone's having a tantrum around here it's going to be me.

Veg man and Emily from F&F. It's not fair. I know that woman. She's pretty, sweet, stylish and considerably younger than me. Of course, she would be his girlfriend. Even the thought of my new career doesn't help. It seems so exciting and is the best opportunity I've had in a long time but something is preventing me from being excited about it and it's not just the betrayal of Veg man.

I never had the illustrious career I always promised myself when I was at school. I wanted to work in television or be a supermodel. Failing that, I was going to travel the world or be a reporter or something. I would be successful and impressive and my life was going to count for something. In my eyes, you only get one life and there is no rewind button on it.

I was going to make it count so the fact that I fell at

the first hurdle surprised even me. When I married Robert and started a family, it appears that I forgot to pack my ambition when I left home and moved into the two bedroomed flat with him.

Now I have the chance to make something of Amanda Swallows. Do I really want to give up on the girl I once was and accept the woman I became? The girl in me was bold, courageous and saw the world as a place with adventure and possibility. The woman in me sees the reality and is grateful for the small pleasures that make every day semi-bearable. Once again that little voice in my head refuses to stop saying, *'I want more from life.'*

The door crashes open and Saskia races in full of something that's obviously causing her much excitement. She drops the bag to the floor and looks at me with her eyes sparkling. "You'll never guess. Eric Conners has broken up with Mae Barnes and word is he wants my Snapchat! Oh my god, he's so fit and if this pans out, I'll be the envy of the entire year. This could be it, my first boyfriend!"

Shaking my head, I try to understand what she's just said. "So, did he ask for your… um… Snapchat?"

She fixes me a disdainful look that shows once again I know absolutely nothing. "Of course not, don't be stupid. He'll probably ask around for a bit then casually throw it into the conversation at break one day. I mean, he's never even spoken to me before so it won't happen overnight."

Her face lights up. "I know, I'll post some new photos on Instagram of me looking super-hot to seal the deal."

She rushes upstairs and I shake my head anxiously. Hot photos on Instagram? Now I'm worried. What sort of photos? Could someone see them and start stalking her? Will they be respectable and not, dare I say it, pornographic?

What should I do? Do I inform Robert that his daughter is posting sexy images on the world wide web and get him to put his foot down and be the bad guy? It has to be him because I have to live with her and it's not worth falling out with her and expect an easy life.

Maybe I should Google my question. It seems to know everything. There must be a forum somewhere on *'help my child's an Instagram porn star.'*

The door opens again and Ryan slouches in and throws his bag on top on his sisters. He just grunts and heads towards the kitchen and I follow him a mass of questions and fear of the unknown.

As he raids the fridge, I try to talk to him.

"Ryan, do you have Instagram?"

He grunts which I take to mean yes. "Can people see your pictures even if you don't want them to?"

He shakes his head. "Depends on your privacy setting. Mine's public."

I feel faint but have to ask, "Um… what about your sister, does she have it?"

He nods. "Unfortunately."

The worry is causing me to almost combust on the spot as I say shakily, "Um… is hers public, do you know?"

He shakes his head. "I don't know, it's not as if I care anyway."

He stalks off with half the contents of the fridge leaving me to reach for my phone and frantically look in the App store. I need Instagram and fast.

One hour later and I think I've downloaded it and set up my account. I've called myself Brandy and found a cool picture of Justin Bieber to act as my profile picture.

It took me a while to figure it all out but now I'm good to go.

I managed to find the kids profiles but held off requesting to follow them. It would look too suspicious so I set about following everyone else I can in the meantime. I manage to get on Zoella's page and try to find pictures similar to hers to post on mine. I'm so engrossed in it I don't notice that it's well past tea time and so put it reluctantly away and set about grilling some fish fingers and throw in some oven chips.

I'll carry on with my Instagram stalking later when they are back in their rooms doing god only knows what – well, God and the whole of cyberspace, anyway.

Saskia is in a good mood for once so I push away my anxiety and enjoy seeing the daughter I love re-surface from the troubled teenager. She laughs and jokes and even throws me the odd smile now and again. Ryan just eats and then leaves almost immediately and once again I'm filled with anxiety at his state of mind. He never talks much and who knows what's going on inside that battle worn head of his. It's at times like these that I curse Robert for ditching his family in favour of a mid-life crisis. We don't have time for those when we have teenagers to worry about.

To my surprise, Saskia clears the table and then looks at me with an uncharacteristically soft look.

"Do you want me to do your make-up, mum?"

I almost drop the plate I'm washing and look at her in surprise. "Ok, yes, thanks."

She looks at me critically.

"Yes, I think you need your eyebrows shaped and you could do with a translucent primer and some contouring. Leave it with me and I'll get everything ready. Meet me upstairs in five minutes."

She heads off leaving me in shock. An invitation to hang out with my daughter. This is unexpected. Well, all the time she's torturing me with make-up she's not posting porno shots of herself on the web.

By the time I reach her room she's ready and waiting. Laid out before me are a set of products that would rival any beauty shop. I think she has the whole contents of Superdrug in this room. I look in disbelief at the array of products designed to confuse and intimidate the uninitiated into this world of beauty.

Saskia pushes me down into her chair and looks at me critically.

"Hm, this will be tough but I'm sure I have the solution."

What solution? Old age, middle-age, past the point of no return age or make me look younger in five excruciating steps? I feel very inferior at this moment in time and shrink into my seat with the embarrassment of someone who knows she's past her prime.

Saskia starts working on the impossible and I settle back in resignation. I decide this is the perfect opportunity to delve into her psyche although I may wish I'd never tried if I don't like what I find.

I cough nervously. "So, how are things?"

She shrugs. "Usual. School's boring and I hate everyone. Except for Eric Connors, of course. I wonder when he'll ask for my Snapchat?"

I feel the anxiety return as I ask matter-of-factly. "So, um... did you post those photos on Instagram yet?"

She grins. "Yes, it's that bikini shot of me last summer. I'm sure that will do the trick."

Now I feel faint and say with concern. "Do you think that's such a good idea? I mean, who knows who looks at these photos and you hear all sorts of stories about weirdoes stalking poor unsuspecting teenagers like yourself."

She rolls her eyes and looks at me with a pitying look. "Maybe if I wasn't PRIVATE! You know mum, don't ask questions about things you know nothing about. I only show what I want anyone to see. I'm not stupid you know. Unlike Diane Turner who posted a picture of her naked and then wondered why Stuart Redfield asked if she wanted to have sex with him."

She laughs but I'm now crying inside. This is way over my head. Naked pictures, near naked pictures, young horny teenagers unleashing their sexuality on the web with no understanding of its implications. This is an epidemic.

Saskia frowns. "You know, maybe Botox would work. I mean, you have quite a few lines on your forehead and are those crow's feet around your eyes? Maybe you should drink more re-energising water to feed your skin."

I couldn't care a crow's feet about my skin at this moment. I'm just surprised I don't look like one of those dogs that's a mass of wrinkles. My worry lines must be off the scale after the day I've had.

I feel a bit miffed about the Botox comment though. I mean, it's not as if I haven't googled it myself but I would never actually have it done. You hear such horror stories and I've watched enough embarrassing bodies episodes to see what really happens when you interfere with nature.

I change the subject back to one I know will make me feel instantly better. "So, tell me, what are the arrangements for the wedding?"

Saskia groans. "I don't want to talk about it. God only knows what's possessed daddy lately. Why is he marrying the bride of Frankenstein in surely what is the most macabre themed wedding in history? The fact he's dragging us into it is astonishing. Surely, he must realise it will be an extremely emotional time for Ryan and me and he's lucky we've agreed to go at all."

I say softly, "Don't you like Lucy?"

She rolls her eyes. "She's ok, I guess. I mean, her make-up is seriously weird and her fashion sense too goth for my liking. She always seems out of it though and doesn't really have too much to say past the battle of waterloo - which I believe she did a thesis on at uni."

I look at her with interest. "So, do you think she's on something then?"

Laughing, Saskia touches up my contour lines and pulls a face.

"Who knows? Dad certainly must be if he's agreed to the weirdest wedding in history. Remind me never to get old. You're all insane."

I look at her and say sadly, "You don't get a choice I'm afraid. It's up to you how you do it though. I just hope you meet your soulmate and grow old happily together. It's a long road to travel, and it helps if you do it with someone who wants to go where you're going. That's all I want for you and Ryan. To be happy and fulfilled and get the most out of life."

She rolls her eyes. "Well, of course, I'm going to be rich and marry someone who looks like Justin Bieber. We'll live in a mansion like the Kardashians and you can look after the kids while we go on holidays and blog our way around the world for free. It's a growing industry you know and if you're lucky, you never have to do a day's work in your life."

Now I know I'm old. I'm so way out of my depth here. I need to get inside this world and fast if I'm to help my children transition into well-rounded adults. This is now a crisis and I don't know what the hell to do next.

After worrying myself stupid through the next thirty minutes, I am absolutely astonished when I see the results of Saskia's handiwork. She smiles and spins me around to face the mirror.

"Tada! The new you in a thirty-minute makeover."

Blinking in total shock, I look at the woman I once was staring back at me. I'm not sure how she's done it but my daughter has worked a miracle. I look ten years younger and dare I say it, almost beautiful.

She smiles. "You look great, mum. Now, all you need is to get to the hair dressers and get some low lights on top of a different set of highlights. A good blunt cut would also take years off you and I'm sure I have a product somewhere for restoring the shine to your hair."

She starts rummaging around in her cupboard leaving me to just stare at the person I've become. She is still there. Lying behind the worry and fears and buried under years of self-doubt and the problems that come with responsibility is the old me, Amanda Swallows. Maybe now is the time to tread the path I wanted to all those years ago. I'm not lying when the thought of caring for my daughter's children didn't fill me with horror. No, it's about time to wake up and smell the roses. I've only got half way in life and the next half will be the best yet. I am finally free to be the woman I should never have turned my back on. This is my time now and the only problem standing in my way is what on earth to do with the rest of my life?

CHAPTER 9

A few days later when I'm at work, trying not to stare in unreciprocated lust at Veg man, that my life changes – finally.

I've already told Susan that I'll join the management training programme so of course, I have already taken the first steps to fulfilment. As I look up, I see my mother has joined the long line of customers queuing at my checkout.

She looks excited about something and I wonder what last minute holiday she's booked, as that's the usual reason for her animation these days.

By the time she reaches the front of the line, my curiosity is off the scale. She grins excitedly and lowers her voice.

"Listen, honey, we don't have long. You know I sent out a tweet about opportunities for you the other day."

I groan inside. Oh no, what has she done?

She grins. "Well, one of my contacts has told me about a super exciting proposition for you. I'm almost tempted to do it myself but I had already booked a week in Sardinia with the WI."

Now I'm curious and say softly, "What is it?"

She leans closer and says, "You need to take next week off work because if you get the job you'll be heading off to Orlando for a week."

What?!!! I look at her in confusion. "What are you talking about?"

I can see the next customer looking impatient as I have stopped scanning and they are getting annoyed. My mother winks.

"I'll meet you when you finish and we'll take it from there. Meet me in the clothing department. I'll have a coffee while I wait for you."

She heads off leaving me a mass of worry and anxiety. This doesn't sound good – at all.

One hour later and I almost run to the clothing department. I almost miss her but then notice my mother struggling beneath a wall of clothes.

She thrusts the garments at me as I approach and says breathlessly, "Here, try these on and I'll fill you in while you get changed."

I don't have time to speak as she pushes me quite forcibly towards the changing rooms.

As I change into some smart clothes, she says with excitement. "One of my contacts works at a magazine. She saw my tweet and personal messaged me about an opportunity that's a bit last minute but perfect for you in every way. Ryan and Saskia will be away for the week and all you need to do is swap your shifts here. The interview's this afternoon and we should get a move on if you don't want to be late."

I almost scream with frustration. "What is it?"

She laughs excitedly.

"They need someone to go to Orlando as a secret holidaymaker. Isn't that the most exciting thing ever?"

I don't think I've heard her right. "What are you talking about?"

She races on. "Well, the person who was going has pulled out at the last minute and they're desperate. All you have to do is pretend to be on holiday and test out the facilities in secret. You know, a sort of undercover travel spy. It's absolutely perfect. Everything is paid for and all you have to do is show up and enjoy. You get a week away for free because absolutely everything is included and all you have to do is file a report when you get home. I'm not going to lie, this is an opportunity that you can't possibly ignore. You need a break my darling and what better way than this? So, make yourself look smart and I'll cover the cost and we'll head over there now. They need to wrap this up today because you leave on Saturday morning."

My head just spins with shock as I try to make sense of what I've just heard. A free holiday, abroad and in America. Wow! I've always wanted to go there and could never afford it. This is a dream come true and my mother's right, I can't possibly turn this opportunity down.

Suddenly, a feeling comes over me of pure excitement. I want this. In fact, I don't only want this, I need it. This is the opportunity I've been looking for. My chance to break out of the ordinary and into the extraordinary. Finally, I can do something different and totally against the safe life I've always lived. This will be an adventure and just like Shirley Valentine, I will rediscover myself. I think this is it. This is just what I've been waiting for. There is a fork in the road and I'm veering off left. Wherever it leads me will change my life. I just know it.

In no time at all, we are waiting in the reception of a smart set of offices in town. "Agora Publications" glows like a neon beacon of future fulfilment behind the receptionist's head. It's all very smart and I'm glad my mum persuaded me to wear the stylish navy suit with peplum jacket and crisp white shirt.

I'm thankful that I took Saskia's advice and had my hair cut into the sharp new blunt cut that just touches my shoulders and the new highlights takes years off me. I have also taken to wearing my make up as she showed me so I'm feeling quite good about myself for once.

My mother is reading a complimentary copy of Cosmo but I'm too nervous. The last interview I had was for Tescos and that was easy as pie. All I had to do was fill out an online form and when I got called in for the interview stage, it was more a 'when can you start?'

I appear to be the only candidate unless they have already been interviewed and I fiddle with my hands nervously.

We must wait for about twenty minutes before the receptionist looks at me and smiles.

"They're ready for you. Take the third door on your left. It should say 'Interview in progress' on the door of room 3."

I smile nervously and my mum whispers, "Good luck, darling. You can do it."

I swallow hard and take the short walk towards opportunity.

By the time I reach the door, I feel a panic attack coming on.

Swallowing hard, I try to steady my nerves. What's the worst that can happen? I don't get the job. It's no big deal, I have a new opportunity already waiting for me. This is just an add-on after all.

So, I steel myself and knock loudly on the door and venture inside.

There are two people in the room sitting behind a long table. They smile at me welcomingly which settles my nerves – just a little.

One of them stands up and offers me her hand.

"Welcome, Amanda. It's so good of you to come at such short notice."

I shake her hand and repeat the gesture with the other lady. I'm not sure why but they look kind of relieved and I wonder why.

The first lady waves towards the seat in front of them and says softly. "Take a seat and we'll get started. So, I believe you know what the job involves?"

I nod. "I think you need a secret holidaymaker to test out the facilities in Orlando."

The second lady nods. "Yes, that's it in a nutshell. The lady that we had lined up has pulled out at the last minute for... um... personal reasons and left us with quite a dilemma on our hands. Are you able to leave this Saturday and spend a week away?"

I nod as the other lady smiles. "Good. Do you have a current passport?"

Once again, I nod and watch as they share a look of relief. Gosh, they must be desperate.

Lady number one smiles happily. "Then we won't beat around the bush, you've got the job. All we need is for you to fill out some personal details and we will hand you the brief to take home with you. Have a good read through and if you have any questions at all, please give either myself or Vanessa here a call."

I smile and say nervously, "I'm sorry, I didn't catch your name."

She laughs and rolls her eyes. "Goodness how rude of me. We were so quick to sign you up all the usual formalities went out the window. My name's Janet Mitchell, and this is Vanessa Michaels. We head up the travel division of Agora Publishing and are responsible for deploying our secret agents in the field and making sure the articles are ready for print."

She leans forward and grins. "Just think of us as Moneypenny 1 and 2 and you won't be far wrong."

They laugh and I join in, totally overwhelmed by what's happening. Wow, travel secret agent. Who even knew there was such a job? I feel super important and almost as if I'm licenced to kill. This is certainly different.

I notice that Vanessa looks a little nervous and points at something on the clipboard in front of her. Janet just shakes her head and says dismissively. "Oh, that can wait. We'll fill Amanda in on the finer details when everything's in place."

Vanessa almost looks relieved and then Janet says briskly. "Right then, if you will just fill in these forms, I'll make sure everything's up to date our end. If you could pack for one week away, we'll send a car for you on Saturday at 9am. The flight leaves at 1pm which should give you ample time to check in and shop in the duty-free."

She winks. "There are lots of perks to this job, Amanda. Who knows, if you like it there may be many more holidays where this is coming from."

I can't believe my luck. Endless holidays all around the world with all expenses paid. Maybe Saskia was onto something. It's not blogging but may as well be. This is a dream come true.

Once I've filled in the paperwork, Janet hands me a folder with all the necessary details. "Here you go, Amanda. All that remains is to wish you bon voyage and a safe and pleasant trip."

She stands and shakes my hand, quickly followed by Vanessa.

As I turn to leave, Janet says quickly, "Oh, I almost forgot to mention, you won't be going alone."

I turn back quickly and see the anxiety in Vanessa's eyes. I knew they'd be a catch, it's obvious by their expressions. I look at them questioningly and Janet coughs nervously. "Um... you will be accompanied by our resident Journalist and photographer. He'll meet you at the airport and will know what to do. Don't worry about him, he'll probably do his own thing, anyway."

She laughs nervously. "I mean, we wouldn't expect you to head off without protection, would we?"

Vanessa laughs a little too hysterically for my liking and I know something's not quite right here. I say nervously, "Um... what's his name?"

Janet looks down at the paper in front of her and says quickly, "Let me see, who have we got going this time? Ah yes, Edward Bastion."

She looks up. "Oh, he's fine. No problem with him, hey Vanessa?"

Vanessa appears to be turning a curious shade of pink as she stutters, "One of our best, isn't that right, Janet?"

They nod their heads vigorously but I'm not that stupid. Whoever this Edward guy is there's something they're not telling me. Oh, well, like they said, he'll probably go off and do his own thing, anyway. It's only a week after all. What could possibly go wrong?

CHAPTER 10

Tina actually screams down the phone when I ring to tell her the good news. "Oh my god, Amanda, that's amazing. You're so lucky. I wish things like that happen to me."

Laughing, I roll my eyes. "Well, it's not as if you won't be going anywhere. It's the same week as you're in Antigua. Come to think of it we're all away. Mum's in Sardinia with the WI. Your children are in Spain with your parents and mine in France with Robert. Who could have seen this coming a week ago?"

Tina laughs happily. "We need to set up Skype as a matter of urgency along with WhatsApp. We can communicate from our bases around the world. I can't wait to hear what it's like being a travel secret agent."

I laugh but then it dawns on me that I have absolutely nothing to wear.

"Tina, I need a new wardrobe and fast. We've only got three days and I've got absolutely nothing to wear except a couple of pairs of shorts, t-shirts, and a kimono. What am I going to do?"

There's a brief silence and then she says excitedly, "No problem. Meet me at the charity shop first thing tomorrow morning. I have a stash of designer gear that I've squirrelled away which will do the job perfectly. All we need is a donation to our worthy cause and you're good to go. When you return, you can donate them back again. It's a win-win situation."

Even though it feels a little strange to be kitting myself out via the charity shop, I realise that beggars can't be choosers so I say gratefully, "Great, you're a lifesaver. I'll meet you there at 10. I'm not due in to work until the afternoon so it works out perfectly."

Tina says in a worried voice, "Were they ok with you taking the time off at such short notice?"

"Yes, I just swapped shifts with Sadie Brown. She wanted some extra shifts, and I said I'd fill in for her when she has knee surgery next month. It's worked out rather well, actually."

Tina sighs with relief. "Good. Are you still starting as a trainee next month?"

"Yes, maybe this is just what I need before I start full-time. It's going to be quite full on for a while so this holiday could be just what the doctor ordered."

She laughs happily. "Good. Then it's all systems go. What about the kids, have you told them?"

My heart sinks. "No, I thought it best not to. They've always wanted to go to Orlando and if they knew I was going when they are in wedding hell, I would never hear the last of it. I'm just going to tell them I'm having a few days away in the Lake District. I think that's the safest bet because Saskia hates walking and Ryan would hate the lack of Wi-Fi. What they don't know won't hurt them."

She laughs. "Your secret's safe with me. Don't worry, they'll never know."

As I hang up, I hope she's right. If they ever found out I was on an all-expenses-paid trip to Orlando, I would never hear the last of it. No, it's much better this way. Like Tina said, they will never know.

Luckily, we are so caught up in making sure the kids have everything for France the conversation is dominated by their trip. They would never ask me my plans because it would never cross their minds that I would do anything different. I don't think they care either. They're so wrapped up in their own lives they don't stop and look at what's happening around them. I could go on Britain's Got Talent and sing the Birdie song and they probably wouldn't know. If I posted a blog post about the latest make-up product or video game, they would take notice. How different things are now from when I was young. Was I ever as selfish as them? Probably, I just never realised it at the time.

The next day I am bright and early at the charity shop and itching to start rifling through the carrier bags of designer blissdom.

Luckily, Tina is there already and hurries me to the room at the back of the shop. She thrusts a couple of carrier bags at me and winks.

"Here you go. There's some great stuff in there. Take it home and use what you want. Just wash it before bringing it back and I'll eBay it on behalf of the charity shop."

I glance inside the bag and almost pass out with shock. Sitting on the top looks to be a Chanel scarf. As I pull it out from the bag, I notice the label and Tina laughs softly.

"It's insane, isn't it? The things some people give away."

I nod in total shock. "Why don't they just eBay it like you're going to do?"

Tina shrugs. "Because it means the same as you donating a M&S jumper. Some people have more money than they know what to do with and they wouldn't even consider selling it on eBay. They don't need to. I suppose their fortune is the charity shop's gain. Without the 'perfect people,' the more deserving among us wouldn't get the help they need. Ms Perfect feels she's doing her duty, and the charity gets to help out more people as a result."

As I replace the scarf in the bag, I look at Tina gratefully.

"I'll look after them, I promise."

She smiles softly. "I know you will. Just remember to have an amazing time and I'll chat with you on Skype from Antigua."

She looks excited. "I actually can't wait to get on that plane. It feels as if Derek and I are strangers these days. He comes home late and goes early. When he's at home, he falls asleep watching the TV and I can't actually tell you the last time we had a meaningful conversation."

She shakes her head sadly. "You know, it's all well and good having money but it comes at a high price. He works so hard he misses out on the little pleasures of life like family time and spending time with the kids. It won't be long before they are off our hands and he will wonder where the time went."

I nod in agreement. "I feel the same. It's ok for me, I see them every day. Robert sees them once in a blue moon and I'm not sure if he's registered they are becoming distanced from him emotionally. I worry about Ryan because he must miss him the most. Living in a house with two women must be difficult and it's not as if I understand a thing about the life they all lead."

Tina shakes her head. "I'm with you there. Croydon is luckier than most, at least he has his father within shouting distance. Derek doesn't understand Sutton at all. She's one of those conundrums he has yet to figure out. I'm not sure many men ever do crack the female code, really."

Laughing, I look at my watch and sigh.

"I'd better be going. I have to get to work and I'm due to pick up my dollars from the bureau-de-change before I start."

Tina looks excited. "So, tomorrow's the day. The children get dispatched to France and Spain and we get to rediscover our youthful selves. Good things do come to those who wait, obviously. Then, when we return relaxed and refreshed you get to start your new life in management and I get to ease back into the role of overstretched wife and mother."

I smile gratefully and give her a hug. "Thanks, Tina. I won't forget this."

She laughs softly. "Just make sure you leave your inhibitions behind and go wild in Orlando. This is your time and you shouldn't waste a minute of it."

As I head off to work, I feel a shiver of excitement run through me. She's right, I'm not going to waste a minute of this opportunity. Orlando won't know what's hit it.

CHAPTER 11

This is it! I feel more nervous than I have ever felt in my life before. It feels almost as though I'm running away because for some reason, I have packed a whole load of guilt in my luggage.

I managed to help the kids pack for their trip and avoid questions about my own plans. It wasn't difficult as they weren't that interested, anyway.

Once I had dealt with the tears and the tantrums and made sure they packed suitable clothes and had enough toiletries, I waved them goodbye with a sigh of relief.

Then as soon as the car turned out of the road, I was up those stairs two at a time as usual and furiously packing whatever I could lay my hands on that passed as summer wear.

The charity shop clothes were amazing, but I still needed swimwear and basic items. I even resorted to rifling through Saskia's wardrobe and just hope she doesn't ever find out I borrowed several items of her clothing.

My nerves are off the scale and I'm not sure I slept a wink all night. This is the strangest experience of my life and I've given birth – twice!

The taxi arrived bang on time and I was soon walking along the travellator to the airport wondering how my mind was possessed so quickly. This isn't me. Amanda Swallows mother of two and abandoned wife doesn't run off to foreign countries with a stranger.

This shouldn't be happening but as I see the signs pointing to the check-in desk, I realise there will be no turning back when I get there.

What if the man's a psycho, and this was all a plot to lure some unsuspecting gullible female into a sex trap? Gosh, one can only hope!

I head towards the line for check-in and look around, wondering if my companion will be holding a sign up to locate me. All I can see are other travellers chatting excitedly in the lines and looking as if they do this sort of thing every day.

I'm not sure what I should do. I don't have any travel documentation, just my passport. They just told me to meet him at the airport but that was all. I decide to stand to the side and wait. I'm sure he'll find me.

As I wait, I check out the other passengers. They seem ok and not the sort that would smuggle a bomb on board. Not that I'm sure that would be obvious but you never know.

I've actually never flown before. I've only got my passport because Robert had told me he was booking us a holiday to Tenerife two years ago as a treat. The trouble is, he ended up going with Lucy because he fell in love with her shortly afterward.

Oh well, lucky me, at least it happened for a reason because here I am now.

Suddenly, I notice a rather large man standing nearby wearing a pale pink shirt with strange matching pink hair. He is shouting quite loudly and the faces of the people he's addressing almost makes me laugh. I listen in with interest.

"So, you live in Yorkshire, do you? Well, you're lucky because I'm betting your house is worth considerably less than mine."

The people's faces are a picture of bewilderment as he shouts, "You see, I live in London and our houses are worth way more than yours. You couldn't possibly afford to live in London you know. You don't realise just how rich you need to be to be able to afford property in London."

Ok, this is embarrassing. What a first-class idiot. The people look quite shocked and I squirm with embarrassment. Ugh, this had better not be Edward Bastion. I have a funny feeling it is though. Maybe this is why the two moneypennies looked so furtive. Anybody facing a week with this pink idiot would surely cancel.

I move away surreptitiously before he can see me. If it is him, then I'm staying put.

As I move away, I notice a man arguing with the agent at the ticket desk. Gosh, people are very irate at the airport. This man looks as if he's about to kill the poor guy. I can't hear what he's saying but the polite, professional, calm, disposition of the handling agent is a credit to the company he represents. I would so hate to work here. I get my fair share of irate customers but they are soon gone. I think I would fear for my life if I worked among this bunch of maniacs.

I have to admit the guy is quite sexy though. He is tall and dark and looks good enough to eat in his smart jacket and chinos. He has that designer beard the men are all wearing these days and under any other circumstance, I would be fantasising about my new life with him. The trouble is, he looks like an angry Ross Poldark on speed, so with a deep sigh I turn away and look around me once again.

I see a smart man in a suit queuing at the first-class desk and my stomach lurches with sudden hope. He looks quite dashing and successful and looks to be about my age, give or take a few years. He looks polished and self-assured, just like a well-seasoned traveller. Yes, that must be him.

I feel the relief grip me as I edge towards him. Yes, this is Edward Bastion, I just know it.

I watch as he checks in his bag and looks around him with an air of boredom. He catches my eye and I smile hopefully.

The check-in agent says something and his attention is taken away so I wait patiently for him to finish and come over.

All of a sudden, I feel a sharp tap on my shoulder and a deep voice say, "You must be Amanda."

Startled, I turn around and feel my face fall as I see angry man standing behind me looking, well – angry.

He looks me up and down and says irritably. "Well, at least you're older than the last one. That's something at least."

Taking a step back I look at him with shock. Oh no, please God, why are you so cruel?

His eyes glitter and he says with exasperation. "Look, there's been a mix up with the reservations. I've tried to sort it out but the imbecile behind the desk couldn't deal with a cat in a birdcage. Now I'm afraid you're going to have to sit in economy."

Somehow, I manage to speak and say with surprise. "Oh, you must be Edward. I'm Amanda."

I offer him my hand but he ignores it totally and says wearily, "I think we've gathered that much already. Anyway, here's your ticket you'll need to check-in at the economy desk. I'm heading to first-class so make sure you get to the gate on time and remember to keep on checking the screens. I'll see you at the other end in the baggage hall."

Ok, I'm speechless. How rude is this man? I don't think I've ever met anyone as rude as him in my life. There are no pleasantries with him. He's cold, abrupt and despite being attractive it counts for absolutely nothing when his piggish personality shines through it. I can see why the moneypennies were nervous. Who on earth wants to spend any amount of time with this... person!

He thrusts the paperwork in my hand and without another word heads over to the first-class check-in desk. I feel the tears well up in my eyes and struggle to get a grip. This is not what I expected at all. I wonder if I should just leave – *now*. Any excitement I may have had has evaporated in a cloud of disappointment. How will I survive with him for one day, let alone one week?

Then something snaps inside me as I see him place his suitcase on the weighing machine. Fine. If this is how he wants to play it, it's fine by me. Two can play at this game and I'm not going to let him ruin my chance of a lifetime. With determination, I join the line for economy. I'm going to make this trip the best one I've ever had and to hell with him. He can run and keep up because he is not going to spoil this for me. Edward Bastion is about to discover that some women bite back and what better one than a mother of two teenagers from hell. This will be a piece of cake compared to living with them.

Now all I've got to worry about is that I'm not sitting next to pink haired man.

CHAPTER 12

I don't even see Edward again because by the time I reach the gate the passengers are boarding already. Knowing him he's already on board guzzling the free champagne and throwing angry glares at the other passengers and crew. Despite feeling a bit miffed that I was given the economy seat, I'm actually more than happy to spend eight hours away from him.

Thankfully pink-haired man is nowhere to be seen either and I pray he is somehow next to Edward in first-class. I doubt it though but a girl can dream.

As it happens, I am sitting next to a charming couple from Surbiton who look normal and turn out to be great company. It turns out they own a villa in Kissimmee and come over three times a year. By the end of the flight, we've swapped numbers and they've promised to do me a deal if I want to stay there in the future. We've also agreed to meet up in Kingston one evening for Tapas when we get back. They have a large circle of single friends who they think would love to meet me.

I knew that travel would broaden my mind. I've

already made new friends and one enemy and I haven't even got started yet.

As we touch down in Orlando, I feel excited. This is it. I'm here in America! The land of the free and that is now me.

I walk with the other jaded passengers towards passport control. Even the air smells different and I look around me with interest. I can't believe I'm here. Things like this don't happen to people like me. I should be at home doing the ironing and planning the weekly shop. Not jet-setting with the perfect people to foreign shores.

The line for passport control is confusing. By the time I've negotiated the automated checkpoints and joined another long line to be allowed in by a customs officer, I'm starting to feel the strain. This has been a very long, trying day already, and it's starting to take its toll.

I feel a flash of irritation as the border official smirks at my name and the rather crazy picture in my passport. I was rushing to get to the dentists when I had this taken and was feeling rather fractious. It's not the best shot of me I'll admit but the laughter in his eyes causes my feathers to ruffle.

So, I'm already wound up when I see Edward blooming Bastion waiting by the escalator. Even from this short distance he looks angry. I sigh inside. Why me?

As I approach, he looks at me with an irritable expression "Finally. What did you do, mess up the automated machine?"

Before I can even answer he starts striding off towards baggage reclaim and I have to run to keep up with him. Once again, I try to fight the seemingly ever-present tears. This man is downright horrible. No wonder they were desperate to fill this vacancy. Now I have my own personal reasons to pull out but it's too late for me. Whoever pulled out before me had a lucky escape.

We wait in near silence for our bags and typically his comes off first. He waits impatiently for me to locate mine which turns up a mere twenty minutes after his. He doesn't even help me get it off the belt and my blood pressure is almost at a critical level by the time we head through customs.

I count to ten several times and picture my happy place to balance my mood. In my case, it's slap bang in the produce aisle with Veg man. He wouldn't treat me like this. He would be an angel and offer me his seat in first-class and carry my bags. Trust me to be stuck with the companion from hell.

It must take us a further twenty minutes to reach the car hire desk and by this time I'm about to faint with exhaustion. Travelling is not for the faint-hearted and it appears that Edward likes to do everything at top speed at all times. It's ok for him with his long stride and apparent high fitness. I'm not used to this and feel in dire need of one of those airport buggies that transport the weaker ones around.

Edward argues with the rental agent for about ten minutes before we are directed to the garage where we collect our vehicle. Once again, we take another escalator to the multi-story car park adjacent to the terminal.

Then we walk the length of the rows of the cars while Edward decides which one he prefers.

He finally decides on a white Cherokee jeep and flings his case in the trunk, saying shortly, "I'll leave you to organise yourself while I sort the car out. I'll just check we've got the right paperwork and set up the sat nav."

Once again, he leaves me to heave my case in the trunk and heads to the driver's side, which is on the wrong side, incidentally.

I slam the trunk shut and take my seat beside him inwardly fuming and vowing not to speak one word to him voluntarily. Two can play at being rude and I have learned from the master - Saskia.

So, instead I just look pointedly out of the window and ignore the total stranger beside me. I had hoped we could get to know each other on the flight over. We would discover we had much in common and vow to have the best trip ever. He would fall in love with me, of course and I would be witty and fascinating company. By the end of the flight, we would be best friends and he would be planning to ask me out as soon as we reach the apartment. Then would follow a week of torrid sex and not a lot of work. We would spend a passionate seven days exploring each other rather than the surrounding areas and when we return home, he would ask me to marry him. What a shame that my hopes and dreams have been shattered – again.

The journey to the hotel is awkward because he is apparently very good at ignoring people when he wants to. He turns on the radio and I enjoy listening to the American accent of the presenter and the soft rock ballads that fill my ears with sweet music. I look at the scenery rushing past with interest. Everything is so big and so clean. The small rather dusty streets of England are replaced with much larger ones. Huge billboards advertise what's at the next turning and the sun shines brightly in a blue cloudless sky. I love Orlando. Already I am in love with the place. It's almost as if life takes a step back and sighs with relief in this magical vacation land.

All around me are hotels rising up out of the huge expanse of land that is in abundance here. It appears so clean and tidy and I instantly feel at home. I even forget that I'm ignoring my companion and look at him with excitement.

"This place is fantastic. Have you ever been here before?"

He shakes his head and grunts. "Not here exactly but I've been to Florida several times. It sort of comes with the job."

I smile in a moment of forgetfulness and say softly. "Then you are very lucky."

He shrugs. "If you say so."

I settle back in my chair and refuse to let him dampen my spirits. Just seeing the sun is enough for me. The heat hit me as soon as we left the terminal building. The sort of heat that warms your soul and heals any illness within. The damp weather in England is evaporated in an instant and I instantly feel re-energised.

I am so fascinated by the surroundings that I'm almost disappointed when we turn into the gates of an impressive entrance.

The security guard comes out of his sentry box and Edward informs him we are checking in. With a small salute he directs us to the main reception and I look with excitement all around me. Wow, this place is impressive. Amazing white New England style blocks of apartments surround a huge lake and Palm trees line the side of the immaculately kept grounds. I watch the American flag flying proudly from an impressive white flagpole and fall instantly in love. I want to live here – forever.

The heat hits me again as we exit the car and head inside the reception. All around is a sense of calm and relaxation and my earlier bad mood evaporates to nothing. I'm finally here and it doesn't matter that I'm with a man who irritates the life out of me. He will cease to be of any importance as I embrace the voyeur inside me and live life to the full. For the next seven days, anyway.

I almost don't register anything but my need to explore this magical place. I leave Edward to sort the rooms out and just wander around in a self-satisfied bubble. This is just what the doctor ordered. Thank God for mothers and twitter that's all I can say.

I walk back to the desk and look at Edward and smile. "Well, so far so good. Have you got our room keys? I actually can't wait to freshen up and maybe take a dip in the pool."

He nods. "We're in block A by the Island pool, apparently. We'll drive around there and settle in. I expect you're tired and would like an early night. We can start fresh in the morning."

As I follow him back to the car, I feel the stirring of something deep inside. A premonition? I'm not sure, but something is telling me this week is going to change my life.

CHAPTER 13

You have got to be kidding me! I look at Edward in complete dismay and he looks at me with irritation as I stutter. "What do you mean, we're sharing?"

We are standing at the entrance of what appears to be a very impressive apartment on the top floor of block A. Edward shakes his head.

"What did you expect? You have your own room, of course. There are two bedrooms here, it's no big deal. We only share a kitchen and lounge area, I'm sure you can cope with that."

Shaking my head, I think about the situation I'm in. I try to reason with myself. It's ok. He's right. There are two bedrooms and it won't matter that I have to share a kettle with him. I can spend most of my time in my room, anyway.

Edward throws me a condescending look as he strides towards the far end of the apartment.

"Anyway, I'll take the bigger room and you can have that one overlooking the car park."

I follow him inside feeling a little lost and for some reason known only to the god of stupidity, I follow him into what can only be described as a luxury room overlooking the lake. Wow! This place is pure luxury. I wander around the absolutely huge room, gawping in awe at the size of the biggest bed I've ever seen. There's a huge spa bath in the centre of the room which leads onto a magnificent bathroom area with 'his and hers' sinks. I see a huge walk-in shower at the end and turn to face Edward and shake my head in disbelief. He just stands looking at me with an annoyed expression as he flings his bag onto the bed.

He says slowly as though talking to an idiot, "Your room is at the other end."

He looks at the door pointedly and I feel myself blushing. Why did I follow him in here? He must think I'm an idiot, although the way he looks at me all the time, I know he does.

Backing out of the room, I say nervously, "Yes, um... sorry, of course. Well, have a nice, um... evening."

Cursing myself for not remaining cool and disinterested, I head across the apartment to the room at the rear.

This room is nowhere near as impressive, although still miles better than my room at home. There's a huge bed and a television. A little settee sits in the corner by a built-in wardrobe. Just off the room is an ensuite bathroom, so I have everything I need.

Sitting on the huge bed I try to take it all in. Why am I surprised that Edward took the best room? He obviously expects the best in life and doesn't do anyone any favours. From what I've seen of him, I'd be more surprised if he did.

Suddenly, it hits home. I've done it. I've done something I never thought I'd do in a million years and I've only got seven days to pack it all in. There's no time to lose.

Quickly, I unpack my suitcase and grab my swimming things. Edward can stay in his room if he wants to, in fact, I hope he does because I'm going to the pool. Finally, after twenty years I can be myself again and not care about what anyone thinks. I have no one to answer to and if I want to stay out all night – I can. This feels so liberating. I almost pity Robert getting married again because he will never experience this kind of freedom.

It only takes me five minutes before I grab the spare room key and head out to freedomsville.

Once again, the heat hits me hard and I absolutely love it. Even though it's 6pm local time, my body is telling me it's 11pm at home. Well, who cares about time restrictions now? I'm going to make the most of my time here and that starts now with a swim in the Island Pool, followed by a relax in the hot tub.

As I first thought this hotel is very impressive. Even the walk to the pool is pleasant and I smile at every person I pass. The sounds of people shrieking and splashing greets me as I head down the path towards nirvana.

Luckily, it's not too busy and I shake my towel out onto a bed that's still facing the sun. I have some sunscreen that I apply carefully and then lie back to let my body unwind after the arduous flight. This feels so good and I almost groan with pleasure. I can even put up with angry man if this is the reward I get.

I lie back and listen to the sounds around me. Children splash and couples chat against the backdrop of music belting from the speakers. After a while, I've heated up enough to require a dip in the pool and take my first plunge. Utter, pure unadulterated bliss greets me as I sink into the calming waters.

I notice some young guys playing water polo nearby so swim to the other side near the waterfall. Every pool should have a waterfall, if nothing else it's a feature and makes you feel you're in total luxury. Maybe I should make a note of that for the travel report. After all, I am on business.

Suddenly, a ball lands in front of me and splashes me squarely in the face. Shaking myself off, I grab it and look around for its owner. I see one of the young guys swimming towards me looking apologetic and I just smile and throw the ball back. He catches it and grins, shouting, "Good throw. You wanna be on our team?"

Looking over I can see it's 2 against 3 and laugh. "Sure, why not? It looks like fun."

I swim walk over, which means that my legs walk and my arms swim because I've never been able to swim that well and it makes it look more natural as I move through the water. As soon as I reach the group, my ball catching friend high fives me and says in his American drawl, "I'm Chase and this is Nate."

Grinning, I say confidently, "Amanda."

He laughs as he throws the ball back into play. "Well welcome, Amanda. Your skills are badly needed because we're losing 6 - 4. You could be our lucky charm."

I think we must carry on playing this game of water polo for a good 30 minutes before the other team win by one point. Amid lots of shouting and teasing Chase laughs as he swims over to me.

"Good job, Amanda. We're heading out for a beer now. Do you fancy joining us?"

I laugh self-consciously. "You are very kind but I'm

sure you don't want someone as old as your mum tagging along and cramping your style."

Chase calls over to Nate and the other two guys. "Hey, Amanda's saying no to a beer."

They all start shouting and before I know it Chase has me launched over his shoulder and shouts, "She's now my prisoner and can't say no."

Laughing, I allow myself to be carried from the pool and quite enjoy the experience, really.

The guys grab their towels and then retrieve my belongings and Chase sets me down to towel off. "Come on, it's happy hour at the reception pool. I think there's a barbie later as well."

Throwing caution to the wind I follow them across a bridge over the lake to the other pool. Chase and Nate walk with me and I learn that they are here for the weekend before heading off to uni. They seem interested in my accent and ask me lots of questions about life in England which I enjoy telling them. They want to know how different things are and I tell them about Ryan and Saskia and enjoy hearing their own stories.

In fact, it must be two hours later that I notice the day has turned to night and I have drunk two cocktails and three beers already.

The guys are so much fun and don't appear to mind that I'm way older than them. It doesn't seem to matter as we laugh and joke and I act completely out of character and just have a good time.

The barbie is awesome as they put it and we cram as many burgers and sausages down us as we are allowed.

They are such good fun and even drag a few other groups in for the party. This must be how Americans live. There is no British reserve here. Anyone is fair game and they seem genuinely interested in hearing about everyone's lives. I envy them their free spirits. I wish I was so confident and friendly to everyone I meet. They have certainly taught me a lot already.

When they asked me if I was here alone, I told them I was with my brother. Hopefully, that will keep our secret identity under wraps and explain why I'm sharing an apartment with 'angry' man. If they see us together it will be obvious we can't stand the sight of one another and is, therefore, the perfect cover.

By the time it's 10pm local time my body is giving up on me. Coupled with the alcohol, I am now feeling extremely tired and quite sick actually.

After promising to meet up tomorrow at the games park, wherever that is, for a game of basketball, I leave my new friends and head back to the apartment.

I am thankful to find it in darkness and imagine that Edward has fallen asleep already. I quickly shower and change and then jump into the huge luxury bed and cave into what my body needs – sleep.

CHAPTER 14

It's still dark when I wake up and look across at the clock by the bed. 7am. I feel wide awake because at home it's midday. I notice a sliver of light inching through the curtain and as I draw it back the sunlight floods the room. Of course, blackout curtains must be compulsory in the Sunshine State, otherwise, nobody would ever get any sleep.

Once again, I feel excited and jump out of bed and head to the shower. Maybe I'll head out for a morning stroll around the hotel grounds to familiarise myself with the layout.

Once I've pulled on some shorts and a t-shirt, I venture out of my room.

"Morning, Amanda."

I jump out of my skin and look across the room. Edward is sitting on the couch looking super-hot and rested and is wearing khaki shorts and a white t-shirt. His hair is dishevelled and his designer stubble from yesterday has thickened overnight.

I swallow hard and remind myself that he's the most

arrogant, annoying, man, I have ever met because the man in front of me is the stuff of fantasies.

He looks up and I see the curiosity in his eyes. He looks me up and down which instantly gets my back up and says dismissively, "We'll need to head to the supermarket for supplies. If we grab enough for breakfasts and lunches, we only need to eat out in the evenings. I'm sure, like me, you could use a coffee or an earl grey or whatever it is you like. We may as well go now and then we can start the day's activities."

He stands up and I try not to focus on his rippling body as he moves across the room. Silently, I chant, *'I hate you, I hate you, I hate you!'*

He grabs the keys from the side and smirks.

"Good night was it? You look like you need at least five hours more sleep judging by those bags under your eyes."

'I hate him, I hate him, I hate him!'

Without even dignifying that comment with a response, I grab my sunglasses that cover up a multitude of late nights and flounce outside, leaving him to catch up with me for once.

We travel in silence as I think up twenty ways to murder him without getting caught. It certainly doesn't help that he looks so gorgeous. My mind hates him but my body is telling me otherwise. Damn that HRT. I knew I should have listened to the warnings about it.

Despite the company I'm keeping I enjoy looking at the scenery as we drive. Everything seems so much bigger and cleaner than at home. The grass is immaculate and the flowers everywhere look sculpted and perfect. Nothing appears out of place and the fact that it's so warm already instantly puts me in a good mood.

We locate the local supermarket and I feel a professional interest as we venture inside. It certainly looks familiar but in a different way. The colours are different and it has a different smell to it. Sadly, I realise that I could spend all day in here just wandering up and down the aisles and looking at the different products on the shelves. Then again, I forgot I was with Edward who proceeds to march along in a military fashion throwing various products in the trolley without even asking what I'd like. When he isn't looking, I sneak in a few things of my own like my children used to do when they were little.

I feel a little awkward as we come to pay because I'm sure I should contribute something. The trouble is, I haven't brought much money with me because I don't have much to spare.

The total comes to $200 and I nearly pass out on the spot. What? How much?

Edward tosses his credit card over and I cough nervously. "Um... here, let me pay half."

He looks at me with an amused expression and then barks abruptly, "It's on expenses, didn't they tell you everything was included?"

Feeling my face redden I say matter-of-factly, "Yes, but I wasn't sure if that included supermarkets too."

Throwing me a pitying look he takes his card and bill from the cashier and starts wheeling the trolley out, leaving me to run to catch up with him - as usual.

Once again, he freezes me out and I'm starting to get annoyed. This man is so rude. Surely it wouldn't hurt him to make polite conversation.

Deciding to be the better person I try to make conversation on the drive home.

"So, what are the plans for today?"

He says abruptly. "First we eat, then we head to Little Lake Bryan."

I feel excited already and ask, "What's there?"

He says shortly, "Water skiing."

Well, that's interesting. I've never water skied before and feel quite glad to be learning. Maybe this trip will be the making of me. It's a bit worrying that I'm such a lousy swimmer but I'm sure they'll be a life jacket involved somewhere along the way.

As we pull into the parking bay outside block A, I feel quite excited about the day ahead.

Breakfast consists of a coffee and a bowl of cereal on the balcony. Edward doesn't make polite conversation and just stares at his paperwork the whole time. It doesn't bother me because I just enjoy the peace and quiet as well as the view. I watch as a boat makes its way to the other side of the lake and think what a slow relaxing way of life this is. I could get used to this and wonder if it's easy to emigrate to America. I would love this life for my kids. With a pang, I realise that I haven't checked on them since I got here and decide to WhatsApp them.

I quickly type.

"Hey, how are things?"

Almost immediately Saskia replies.

"Oh, good of you to ask. The fact I'm in hell doesn't seem to matter to you. I've been calling all day and you haven't even bothered to answer."

My heart sinks as I type back.

"I'm in the Lake district and the signal's all over the place. Why, what's the matter?"

"Well, the wedding was surely the weirdest thing I've ever seen in my life. My dress was itching me all day, and I had

nobody to talk to. Ryan's behaving like a total man-whore and I think he got off with half the bridesmaids including Lucy's sister's daughter. I mean, that must now make her his step cousin which is incest, surely? You really should speak to him mum because at this rate he'll catch something."

The words start to swim before my eyes as she carries on.

"Anyway, if you weren't being so selfish and locking yourself away on some remote part of the British Isles, you would have been around to hear my big news."

Now I'm even more worried as the words swim before my eyes.

"I HAD MY FIRST KISS."

Quickly, I punch back,

"Tell me everything, immediately."

This is typical. It was bad enough that I missed her first step when I left her with my mother while I went to the supermarket. Then I missed her first day at school because I was on Jury Service and Robert got to take her. Now this! I'm surely the most terrible mother alive.

I almost can't wait for the words to hit the screen and then I wish I hadn't.

"Oh, mum it was everything I always thought it would be. You know, I really do think that this is fate. I'm so glad I waited because Nicola is everything I ever wanted in life. I never knew love would be this good. Oh, sorry, I have to go. Nicola's here now and we're heading out for the day. Speak soon x."

Ok, I feel ill now. This is huge. This is what happens when you leave your children in the care of clinically insane warriors and jet off with a strange man half way around the world. Not only has my daughter kissed a woman but my son is now officially a man-whore. I picture him as a baby as I held him in my arms and envisioned his future. I remember gazing at him lovingly and whispering that he could be anything he wanted in life. The world was his to take and own but I'm sure 'man-whore' wasn't among the list of options.

I can feel the blood rushing to my head as my world explodes several thousand miles away and I'm not there to deal with the casualties.

There is only one person I can turn to in my hour of crisis so I quickly type a message to my mum.

"Hey, how is Sardinia? Listen, I think we've got a problem. Ryan is now a 'man-whore' apparently and Saskia's dating a woman. Tell me what to do immediately!"

I wait nervously, willing the answer to materialise out of the worldwide superhighway but nothing. I can see the message was delivered but it remains unread.

This is strange. My mum is glued to her phone and can't ignore a notification to save her life. What's going on?

I stare at the screen anxiously but nothing happens. Ok, now my heart is racing and the blood pounds around my head punishing me for daring to think I could have some *'me'* time. People like me don't get to relax and do things the perfect people do. We need to battle our way through life dodging the slings and arrows that life and William Shakespeare throw at us. First my children are in crisis and now it would appear my mother. I am stuck with a man I can't stand in a place I love with all my heart with no way of getting home for the next six days. I knew I should never have thought I could pull this one off. It's all my fault and Robert's for starting this in the first place. If only he had resigned himself to a lifetime of tedium and making the best of what we had. How dare he dream for more from life and walk out that door with no thought of the repercussions? No, this is all Robert's fault and if he was here now, I'd give him a battle re-enactment to make him remember.

Then I hear a terse, "Well if you've finished playing with your phone maybe we can do what we've been sent here to do. I'll meet you by the car in five minutes. Pack your swimwear, you're going water skiing."

CHAPTER 15

The car may as well have been the Tardis because I don't even remember getting to Lake Bryan. I can't stop thinking about what's happening in France and now Sardinia. What if mum was abducted by rebels on her way to the WI retreat? She may have had an accident and is weak and calling for help in some strange lonely foreign hospital. My children are now out of control and my wayward ex-husband is too busy playing soldier to notice. No, this is all my fault and there is absolutely nothing I can do about it.

The car stops and Edward slams the door behind him. Gosh, he even exits a car angrily. I follow suit and then blink as the bright sunlight hits me as it bounces off the white sand. Wow, this place is amazing.

I look around me in awe. Set by the water's edge is a sort of a shack that looks like something from the movies. It's set on the whitest sand that sparkles in the sunlight and it appears to be some sort of beach bar.

Wooden tables and chairs are placed on a sort of wooden raised platform surrounding a bar. Just to the side is a long reception desk where they obviously organise the water sports activities.

I race to keep up with Edward's long strides as he approaches the desk.

As I'd expect, a young guy, who looks way too cool for school, leans nonchalantly. His hair is fairly long and wild, surfer-style and he's wearing lots of those meaning bracelets and a corded necklace. I feel as if I'm on a movie set and feel a shiver of excitement run through me.

As Chase and Nate would say, this place is awesome.

I watch as Edward speaks to the surfer dude and then they head over toward me. The guy smiles and winks.

"First time, hey?"

I nod nervously and watch as he laughs to himself and heads towards the water's edge where it looks like a speed boat lives.

Now I'm having second thoughts and look at Edward nervously.

"Um, maybe it's best if you go first."

He shakes his head and smirks. "I'm not. You're the only one going in today."

What?! I look at him in astonishment and he nods towards his camera. "I'm taking the photos for the article and writing the piece up later. Your job is to be the holidaymaker – remember?"

Swallowing hard, I say in a small voice, "Um... I could always take the photographs. I mean, I'm fairly good with a camera and you would be way better than me on the water. The shots would be much more impressive."

He smirks. "So, you're a photographer, now are you?

And what exactly do you intend on taking them with because if you think I'm letting you loose on mine you're seriously mistaken?"

Ok, now I'm getting just a little ticked off with his attitude and say angrily.

"I'll have you know anyone can take a photograph these days. We all have iPhones you know and you would be hard to get a better photograph than that. Add a few filters and it would rival any 'professional' photo you could produce."

He looks at me incredulously. "An iPhone. Is that the best you've got? Well for your information there is rather a lot more to taking photographs than snapping away on your phone and applying a filter. You stick to what you do best – nothing and leave the professional jobs to those who are."

He starts striding off towards the boat and I think I've hit a nerve. Good! I intend on hitting more than just his nerves before this trip is over.

As I approach the boat, I see the kind smile of surfer dude and sort of relax – a little. This will be fine. I can do this. I mean, how hard can it be? If Edward doesn't get his photographs, then that would be an added bonus and serve him right.

We climb on board the speedboat and I pointedly ignore Edward by sitting as far away from him as a small boat will allow.

I look around me with interest and love how the sun sparkles on the blue of the water and turns it a different shade. This is a little piece of paradise here and I could see myself running such a place in my future. I really must look into the immigration policies when I get home.

The engine starts and soon we start speeding towards the centre of the lake. The wind whips through my hair and I feel exhilarated. I can do this; it's just mind over matter.

As we near the centre the boat slows down a little and I look in the water nervously. Then something catches my eye in the distance and I peer at it a little closer. This can't be right.

I look over to my captain and say slightly hysterically, "Is that a crocodile over there?"

Edward and surfer dude look over and the young man shakes his head. "No, it's a gator. Don't worry though, he'll swim off in the other direction and we'll go the other way."

I catch Edwards' eye and shake my head. "I'm not going in there."

He smirks. "I figured as much. Your sort doesn't mix well with the wildlife."

I look at him in shock. My sort? What on earth is that supposed to mean? If my sort means any sensible, self-preserving mother of two who has listened to all the warnings in televisiondom about never and I repeat never swimming with crocodiles, then yes, I am very much that sort of person.

I feel them both watching me and can tell they think I'm about to fold. Well, I'll show them. I'm not about to let a little thing like a killer reptile get in the way of my holiday. So, I just snort and wave at its retreating figure dismissively. "Well, shows what you know. Kit me up buddy, I'm going in."

Surfer dude, who I should really call Wayne because that's his name, high fives me and thrusts a lifejacket towards me.

"Cool. Put this on and then sit on the edge of the boat. I'll fit your skis and show you what to do."

I pointedly ignore Edward as I do as he says and realise that I have stupidly allowed my pride to place me in the hands of Beavis and Butthead and immediately worry about my own sanity.

Edward for once now looks slightly worried. "You know, you don't have to go through with this, don't you?"

I sneer at him. "That's where you're wrong, Eddie. I think I kind of do because you've obviously formed this opinion of me that I now want to shove back in your face. So, if you'll just shut up and do what you're being paid to do we can get on with this."

The look on his face is reward enough as he looks at me in total amazement. Deliberately, I turn my back on him and then almost faint in shock as I see some sort of eel thing raise its head out of the water nearby.

I start to shake inside and take several calming deep breaths. It's fine, you've got this. Just pretend you're in 'I'm a celebrity get me out of here.' It's an organised activity and no one will die out here. Relax and think of how much you can gloat when this is over.

I'm not sure what sort of Zen-like state I've placed myself in because the next thing I'm aware of is me falling off the back of the boat into the marine life infested water. I find myself clinging to the rope handle for all I'm worth. Oh my god, this is it, I'm actually going to die out here.

Wayne, waves and gives me the thumbs up and I take some satisfaction in seeing Edward looking at me anxiously. Gritting my teeth, I wait for the inevitable mortifying conclusion of this whole exercise as the boat starts to move away and I watch the rope uncoil from the back of it.

I swear its only fear and adrenalin that can be credited for what happens next.

As the boat lurches forward and picks up speed, I brace myself. Then as the rope pulls me upright, I feel as if I can fly. I grip onto the lifeline that will save my life and will myself to stay upright as we skim across the water.

This is it, I'm water skiing. I actually can't believe my sea legs because I am suddenly Amazonian Jane, the ninja water ski warrior. I picture that beast in the waters below and my body locks into place, just the way Wayne described it. I can't believe I'm actually doing this. The wind whips around me and the spray refreshes me as we shoot around Lake Bryan. Wow, I love this. I actually think I can do anything. This is easy.

Inevitably though my strength lets me down and as I catch a particularly nasty bump in the waves from the boat, I feel myself falling into the dreaded water. Almost as soon as I surface, I see the boat heading towards me like a Baywatch scarab and breathe a sigh of relief. Now all I have to do is get into the thing and I will have the coolest story to tell my grandchildren when I'm resigned to looking after them in my future.

Wayne and Edward haul me up into the boat and to my surprise Wayne hugs me. "Wow, honey, you're a natural. Good job."

I can't stop grinning as he helps me remove the skis and jacket and I throw Edward a triumphant look.

"Did you get your photographs?"

He nods, looking quite shell-shocked and says grudgingly. "You did well out there. Although your technique could use a little work."

Luckily, the roar of the engine drowns out the expletives as I am thrown back against the side of the boat. I feel the resentment threatening to drown any good intention I've ever had. This man is now my mortal enemy and all bets are off. He will wish he did have the younger model on this trip because the older one is about to fight back.

CHAPTER 16

We head back to the hotel in silence. I think I'm still in shock because when we returned to the love shack, Wayne rushed in and told everyone about the giant Alligator in the lake. As it turned out, it was an unusual sighting, and they were going to have to call in the professionals to remove the offending creature before any harm was done.

I feel in utter shock that I was placed in danger like that while thinking it was their tame mascot or something.

Edward hasn't spoken to me since discussing my technique and I sit beside him a seething mass of hate and resentment. Goodness, this is only day one. What on earth will I feel like by day seven? One of us may not make it back alive if today is anything to go by.

By the time we reach civilisation I have simmered down a little. As soon as we stop, I rush from the jeep and then hear a loud, "Amanda, I thought that was you. How about that game of basketball?"

Looking over, I see Chase and Nate heading towards

me decked out in their shorts, shirtless and looking like one of those adverts for a gym. I see the shock on Edward's face and giggle to myself. They reach us and I smile happily. "Hey, guys. This is my brother, Eddie."

Once again, the look on his face almost makes me burst out laughing as Chase grins. "Good to meet you, man. Hey, your sister's one cool chick. She can certainly throw a volley so we've drafted her in for a game. You up for it?"

Edward looks totally shell-shocked and I say quickly.

"No, he can't. He's got work to do, haven't you, Eddie?"

He looks between us and narrows his eyes.

"Yes, of course. I'll see you later. Two hours and then we're off again. Don't be late."

He nods to the guys and then heads off inside and Chase looks after him in surprise.

"You're not very alike, are you?"

I laugh softly. "No thank goodness. Anyway, haven't we got a game to win?"

Thank goodness for teenage boys. I spend the next hour in good company and have a great time. I picture the basketball as Edward's head and give it a good pounding. Once again, I surprise my new friends with my ball skills and they treat me to a soda as they call it afterward.

They ask if I want to go with them to Disney Springs, wherever that is, later, but reluctantly I decline. I have to remember I'm here to do a job and as much as I would love to take them up on their kind offer, I must endure another hellish few hours with angry man.

Once I reach the room, I am thankful that Edward is nowhere to be seen. Maybe he's writing his article in his room or swimming in the pool. Grabbing myself a large glass of water I head into my room and reach for my phone. Maybe I should stalk the kids on Instagram to see the evidence of the wedding shenanigans for myself.

Before I can however, the iPad makes that weird skyping noise and I rush to answer it, hoping against hope that it's my mother back from her imprisonment.

I almost cry with relief as I see the welcome familiar face of my friend Tina.

She shouts excitedly, "Oh my God, look at you. What on earth have you been doing?"

Laughing, I realise what a mess I must look after the physical day I've had. As I peer at her I snort, "What about you? Did someone forget to use sunscreen?"

Tina looks redder than Veg man's tomatoes and she rolls her eyes. "Stupid Caribbean sun. Who knew I should have packed factor 50? Factor 15's obviously not up to the job."

I laugh and feel the happiness edging out the anxiety as I relax at the thought, I'm talking to a friendly face for the first time in days.

She smiles happily. "You know, we're having the most amazing time out here. Derek is out of control now we've been let loose on our own. He thinks he needs to pack everything in while we can and I must tell you, I'm absolutely exhausted."

Laughing, I can sympathise.

"Yes, holidays aren't for the faint hearted, are they?"

She nods. "So, tell me about life as a secret holiday-maker. What have you been up to?"

I shake my head sadly. "I'm so glad you called, Tina. It's been dreadful. I feel so guilty that I'm here without the kids, who are way out of control in France, I might add."

She looks concerned. "Why, what's happened?"

I sigh. "Ryan has a new occupation as a man-whore, apparently and Saskia has indulged in her first kiss with someone I'm not sure I should mention."

Tina looks intrigued. "Well, you can't leave it there, who is it? Oh, I know, don't tell me. An older man? One of the waiters? The best man? The possibilities are endless."

I shake my head sadly. "No, none of the above. It would appear that my daughter's first kiss was with a woman."

Tina looks absolutely gobsmacked. "What??? You must be mistaken – surely."

I feel like crying uncontrollably. "It's true. She told me that Ryan's now a man-whore, and she kissed someone called Nicola. She said she was glad she had waited because this Nicola is everything she ever wanted. The trouble is, I'm not even there to offer my motherly advice, and she's just annoyed that I'm in the Lake District. What will she say when she finds out I'm in Orlando without her? She will never forgive me."

Tina looks worried. "Oh my God, that sounds terrible. The trouble is, things are so different now. There are no divisions these days and anything goes. I suppose you could always be grateful that you gain another daughter and not a smelly teenage yob whose feet smell and spits everywhere."

Shaking my head sadly, I say falteringly. "I'm also so worried about my mother. She's not answering WhatsApp, which can only mean she's either dead or in hospital. It's been at least four hours since I messaged her and you know my mother, she hates to see that little red number next to her Apps."

Tina looks even more worried now. "Is there any

other method of communication? You could always try phoning instead."

I nod. "Maybe I'll try later."

She suddenly looks excited. "So, you never told me, who did they send to accompany you? Please say George Clooney and I'll die happy."

I immediately feel my anger returning with a vengeance. Maybe it's because it feels good to chat to someone normal and non-judgemental but I really let rip.

"That's the worst thing about this whole thing. I'm telling you, Tina, this man is something else. I've never met anyone so rude, arrogant and downright nasty as he is. To look at him you'd think he was the catch of the century. I mean, he's not bad to look at I suppose and could in fact be many women's fantasies. However, when he opens that big mouth of his you realise what a total asshole this man really is. In fact, if he was in a field of asses, he would be the biggest one in it. Oh, and don't get me started on his condescending attitude as he looks down at you. He thinks he's above everyone and looks down on the little people as though we're an inconvenience sharing the same air as him. He has no compassion and actually tried to have me killed today."

Tina's eyes widen in total shock and she shakes her head wildly. I shiver. "I know, despicable isn't it. He thought it would be amusing to watch me get eaten alive on camera for his travel article. He was too scared to go in the water himself but I was expendable and the world would obviously be a better place without me in it. Because for some reason my friend, he absolutely hates me and I can tell you it's right back at him, big time."

Tina looks as if she's about to cry and I nod in agreement. "Even you can see what a monster this man is and

I absolutely hate every inch of my body that is wishing he would just pick me up and tie me to his bed and do unspeakable things to me all night. You see, that's the trouble with hormones. They obviously can't be trusted to steer us on the right path of life. No woman in her right mind would want to be saddled with this total creep for even five minutes, let alone forever. God, I hate him."

I watch as Tina is almost crying as she shakes her head wildly and then realise that she's not sympathising with me, she's warning me and a cold feeling creeps over me as I say with resignation, "He's behind me, isn't he?"

She nods, looking mortified and I hear a cough and a terse, "Here, I thought you could use this."

Cringing, I swing one eye towards my right as a Starbucks coffee appears around my right shoulder. Reaching out a trembling hand I grab it and say in a small voice, "Um… thanks."

I hear him leave the room and just stare at Tina with complete and utter mortification.

She laughs softly, "Well, that went well. You're right though, that man is hotter than my sunburn right now and hotter than the embarrassment burning on your face. Whoa I would love to be a fly on the wall when you finish up here. Way to go, Amanda, you've just made your bad situation one hundred percent worse."

I could almost cry and just stare at her in abject horror. "What am I going to do now?"

Tina laughs loudly. "You're a mother, you'll figure it out. You've had years of practice with dealing with emergencies. What woman alive hasn't had to manipulate the situation to get what she wants. It's in our DNA and if you can cope with the teenagers from hell, a hot guy and I mean hot incidentally, won't stand a chance."

She looks at me sympathetically as I hear Derek calling her. "Chin up, Amanda. You'll figure out how to turn it all on him. Your Mum will be fine, she's just probably forgotten her charger and as for the kids, they'll come good. I'm sure Ryan is just doing what every other teenage boy does at this time of his life. He's not stupid, just lucky, I guess. Saskia is probably just winding you up because she knows she can. Now off you go and act as if nothing has happened. Say you were talking about someone else or something. He can't prove anything and if he's a bad as you say he is, who cares what he thinks, anyway?"

She blows me a kiss as she snaps her screen shut. Now I wish the Alligator had eaten me because death by reptile is suddenly a much more attractive proposition than facing Edward Bastion at this moment in time.

CHAPTER 17

I decided to have a shower to wash away my embarrassment and give me time to decide how to play this. This is a nightmare of epic proportions. He hated me before and now he must wish he'd never laid eyes on me. Even pink haired man from the airport would be better than him. He's so thick skinned he would have taken it as a compliment.

Soon I'm ready and feeling like myself again. Now that I'm semi-presentable I wander into the communal area and nervously look around me. I can see Edward sitting on the balcony typing on his iPad and with a deep breath head out to join him.

He doesn't look up and I sigh inside. Oh well, here goes nothing.

Coughing nervously, I say in a small voice, "Um… I'm sorry about my outburst earlier. I've always been a little highly strung. I suppose it's the result of living with two teenagers and being abandoned by my husband. Sometimes it all gets a bit much and I kind of lose it for a moment. I didn't really mean anything I said back there."

He looks up and as our eyes meet, I squirm with embarrassment. He looks at me with irritation and a little piece of me dies inside. This man's a monster – obviously.

Then he nods to the chair opposite and says tersely, "Sit down."

Feeling like a kid in front of the headmaster, I perch on the edge nervously.

He looks at me steadily and then says gruffly.

"I'm sorry, Amanda."

I blink and try to understand what those three words really mean. Sorry for what? Sorry for allowing me to come here in the first place? Sorry for not finishing me off when he had the chance? Sorry for bringing me a coffee in his first act of kindness since we met? Sorry for listening in on my conversation or sorry for breathing.

I say softly, "For what?"

He leans back in his chair and runs his fingers through his hair and looks at me with a vulnerable expression in his eyes that takes my breath away.

"I'm sorry for being the asshole you described. You were right. I deserved every word of what you said and more. If anything, you were being kind."

Ok, now things have just got weird. Who is this man sitting in front of me because whoever he is, he's zillion times better than asshole man?

He smiles and I stare at him in fascination. Wow, that smile has cancelled out the last twenty-four hours in a flash. Gosh, I'm so fickle.

He says sadly. "I think I may have misjudged you."

I look surprised, "Why, what do you mean?"

"When I saw you at the airport, I saw a woman hanging around the first-class desk in her designer clothes looking like she expected the best of everything. I saw you looking at the passengers queuing in economy with horror on your face and I thought you were one of those women who expected everything handed to her on a plate in life."

Ok, now I'm in shock. I croak out, "Me?"

He nods. "I was angry because you were just another in a line of bored housewives looking for a free holiday or more. I've seen them all and spent way too much of my time stuck with them on trips away. The girls in the office are running out of options because I am hard on my companions for a reason."

I look at him with interest. "Why is that?"

He shakes his head sadly and I see a flicker of pain spark in his eyes.

"Because I am angry, Amanda. Angry at life and angry at myself for letting it affect me so badly. I hate the fact that life goes on and people exist in a shallow world when the good among us are taken without warning. I'm angry that I have to exist when it's the last thing I want to do. You see, Amanda, I'm angry for a very good reason. I lost the only person who meant anything at all to me in the most brutal of ways. I carry on because there is nothing else I can do. I'm angry that she left me after a stupid moment of madness and angry because other people live and don't even realise what a gift they have in being able to do so."

I see the pain in his eyes and say softly, "What happened?"

He looks out to the lake and I see the lost look in his eyes and my heart melts.

He sighs. "Karen was my wife. She used to accompany me on all my trips and we started this business together. She was full of life and the funniest person I have ever met. She was also beautiful inside and out and everything I ever wanted. Then one day she went out to get the shopping and never came back."

I think I'm holding my breath as I watch him relive the memory.

"It started to get late, and I was worried. Her phone went to answer phone, and she never picked up. The first thing I knew about it was when there was a knock on the door and the police were standing there. I knew she was dead; it was in their eyes. They told me she must have been changing the channel on the radio, or something ran out in front of her because she misjudged a bend in the road and ploughed into a tree. She was killed instantly. Luckily, nobody else was involved but in that one moment everything changed. She was gone and took my heart with her."

He looks at me and says sadly, "So you see, Amanda, I'm angry for a reason. I'm angry that she lost her life for absolutely no reason at all. If she had been home with me, she would still be here today. If I had gone instead of her, she would still be here today and if she had been concentrating or driving slower, she would still be here today. It angers me way more than you could ever know because I hate the fact that other less deserving people carry on living when such a good person doesn't."

I shake my head sadly. "Life is cruel, we all know that. It's filled with injustice and there's no reasoning with it. Things happen every minute of the day that shouldn't. People die for no reason. Illness strikes down people who don't deserve it. Undeserving people get away with everything good honest people pay the price for and there is no sense in any of it. But somehow, we deal with it in the only way we know how. We carry on because we have no other choice. If you think about it too much, it will destroy you. Things happen and we move on. We leave that little part of us behind and take the rest of us forward with that little piece of us missing. We will always be incomplete because of it but carry on living because we owe it to ourselves and our loved ones to do so. You'll never forget Karen because she lives in your heart and soul. You will always have the soul of an angel accompanying you through life, urging you forward to be the best you can be. You have to let go of your anger though, Edward because it will destroy you. I should know because I've had to start again when I was least expecting it."

He stares at me and then says softly, "What's your story, Amanda? I feel as if I've misjudged you, so now it's your turn to set the record straight."

I smile sadly. "Nowhere near as devastating as yours. My husband left me for another woman but it was inevitable, really. We were never really soul mates, just two people who settled for something they thought they wanted. I can't complain though because we had two children who I love more than life itself. The trouble is, life is hard because now I'm struggling alone and trying hard to keep it all together. My husband married his new love this weekend and my children are with them now. I work in Tescos to get a bit of money to allow us to eat and life is hard. When my mum found out about this opportunity, I seized it with both hands. I've never been abroad before, unless you count the time my husband arranged for us to go to Tenerife. He ended up taking his new wife instead of me though but the sad thing is, I wasn't that bothered. You see, what we had wasn't anything like you describe. We were just friends not soul mates. We existed together because that was all we knew. It took him finding his new wife to realise what we had both been missing out on all those years. I'm happy for them in a weird way and maybe I can find some happiness of my own one day."

I laugh softly and point down at my clothes. "You're right about the designer clothes though. The sad thing is even they aren't mine. I needed some clothes to bring with me and my friend Tina, who you sort of met already, works in the local charity shop. She loaned me these designer clothes as a favour. All I have to do is wash them and take them back ready for her to sell on eBay."

Edward looks astounded and I giggle at his expression.

"So, as you can see, you were way off mark. I was looking in horror at the queue of economy passengers because of a conversation I overheard while I was waiting. Believe it or not, there was a bigger asshole than you on that flight and I was hoping against hope he wasn't my companion."

Suddenly, Edward starts laughing. He leans back in his chair and laughs so hard I think the whole resort can hear him. It's so infectious I join in and we sit on the balcony in a little corner of paradise and laugh ourselves stupid.

CHAPTER 18

Now we've cleared the air things change for the better. We made ourselves a nice lunch and sat on the balcony chatting like we should have done in the first place. It turns out that Edward owns Agora Travel and only occasionally heads off on these trips himself. He has a team of other journalists who jet all over the world writing about it and getting paid by the tour operators to give them a write up. Pure genius.

I tell him all about my boring life which he seems strangely fascinated with.

So, as we head out to explore it's now as firm friends, not enemies. Strange how things work out, really.

As we leave the resort, I look at him with excitement. "I've never been to Disney before, have you?"

He shakes his head. "No, luckily I've always escaped this one. It was never a place I wanted to visit."

Shaking my head, I feel the excitement grip me. "Well, I can't wait. I always wished we could have taken the children when they were small but we never had the money to. I feel I've failed as a parent because they've never had the sort of childhood, I wanted them to have."

Edwards says softly. "It sounds as if you've covered the important stuff. It's not about what you can give them materially, your time and attention is much more valuable. I'm guessing you're the first person they turn to in a crisis and are the most important person in their life. It doesn't matter if you didn't give them the full works, they have a mum who is always there for them and puts their needs above hers. Well, at least I'm guessing, anyway."

Laughing, I tease, "Well, excuse me if I don't trust your judgement. You certainly got me wrong and look what happened there. For all you know, I could seriously neglect my kids and am in fact doing just that now. They think I'm in the Lake District because I was too scared to tell them what I was really doing."

Edward laughs. "So, what do you think they'd say if they knew where you are now?"

"Probably go crazy and call me selfish and embarrassing for daring to think I could have a life outside of the one I have. I'm not allowed to think I could do anything for me anymore. If I do, I'm selfish and desperately trying to hang onto my youth. The sad fact is, they are probably right. Now Robert is gone it's kind of made me look at my life differently. I want to do everything I always wanted to before real life moved in and set up home. This is my big adventure which is why I almost sacrificed myself to the sea monster this morning. I've come to realise that there is no rewind button on life and mine appears to be on fast forward. There's a lot of living to pack into a few short years with no resources to fund it."

The silence hangs in the air but it's not awkward. Now we know more about each other we don't have anything to prove anymore.

As we drive my thoughts turn to my children and my mother and the anxiety returns to punch me hard. I must start shifting nervously because Edward says, "You've gone quiet. Is something bothering you?"

Sighing, I offload yet another one of my problems onto him.

"I'm a bit worried about my mother. She's normally always at the end of her phone and rarely ignores a notification, yet she hasn't replied to my message for nearly two hours. I'm starting to think something's happened."

Edward looks worried. "Is there anyone you can call to check up on her?"

Thinking about it for a moment I can only recall that she went with the WI. My mum has lots of friends but not many close ones.

"I suppose I could contact the WI office and ask if they know where she is. It's a start at least."

Edward nods. "Tell me the details and I'll set the moneypennies on it. There's not a lot they can't discover if they put their minds to it."

Of course, moneypennies. I nod gratefully.

"That would be great, thanks. I don't know why I never thought of it before. They were the reason I got this job in the first place. If they hadn't tweeted about it, my mother would never have found out and bulldozed me into applying."

Edward groans. "I don't want to know. Their business practices are a little unorthodox and I prefer to keep myself in the dark as to how they recruit my latest victim."

He grins and I laugh with relief. Gosh, it's good to have someone to help out. I've forgotten what it's like.

Before long we arrive and I look around in awe. Oh my God, I'm in the Magic Kingdom.

I can't believe that I've finally made it to Disney World. The land where you can wish upon a star and dreams come true. I look around with excitement as Edward looks around with resignation.

"Right then, I've got a map and we can follow it and get some pictures and discover what makes this place tick."

He starts striding up main street and I feel as if I've died and gone to heaven. This place is magical. The little buildings look as if they've been transported from a story book. Cinderella's castle is the stuff of dreams and there is even a show taking place right now on a stage set up before it. I look around me in awe and feel the shiver of childhood expectation returning with a vengeance.

Quickly, I look at Edward and say with excitement. "I love this place already. Why has it taken me so long to get here?"

He laughs and takes a photo of me in front of the castle. "Come on then Princess, let the queuing begin."

He wasn't wrong about the queues. We queue for hours for the rides that everyone is talking about. It's so hot and I feel as if I will melt but that doesn't even matter here. This place is the stuff of dreams and we intend on sampling every treat here.

Edward is good company and poles apart from the angry man of this morning.

I have my photograph taken with various costumed characters and I don't think there's a landmark we haven't captured on film. While we queue, we chat to the others in the line and Edward interviews them for his article. They are only too happy to talk about their trip and recommend places for us to go.

We grab an ice cream as we head to the next ride and something occurs to me.

"You know, Edward, I should use this week to communicate on a different level with my kids."

He looks interested. "What do you mean?"

Holding up my phone, I grin.

"Well, before we left home, I was a little concerned that I know nothing of their media life. So, I opened an Instagram account under the name of Brandy. She loves Justin Bieber the same as Saskia and is into computer games like Ryan. I googled their interests and posted pictures of things I know they like. Well, maybe I should continue to do so and find out what they're into. Most of the time I don't have a clue as they live in their rooms for most of the evening and only venture out for food. This week could change all that. What do you think, it's not considered deceptive is it?"

He looks thoughtful. "I'm not sure it's really that ethical. For instance, you're fabricating a person with the sole intent on spying on your kids. They will tell you things they may not wish you to know and it could all blow up in your face."

I shrug, "Well?"

He grins. "I say bring it on. It's genius. Just make sure you're not in the photos and post what you think interests them."

Grinning, I look around me and then take a quick snap of the castle for Saskia. Perfect.

Soon I have a whole album of photos for Instagram

and decide to post them later when we get to Wi-Fi. This will be fun. It keeps them close in my thoughts in a good way, not a worrying one. This will be the best thing I ever did; sharing my experience with my children without them knowing.

CHAPTER 19

I have decided that everyone should visit Disney world once in their lives at least! This place has it all. Funny little lands that look as if they have jumped straight out of the pages of a storybook. Well-manicured grounds that obviously have no weeds or animals to destroy them. Perfect sunny skies and smiling people everywhere. It's impossible not to fall in love with such a magical place.

The fact that Edward and I are adults on our own doesn't matter here. Lots of adults are here without children and are just reconnecting with their own inner child.

Every little land offers something different and by the time we break for something to eat I am seriously worried about the storage capacity on my phone.

We grab something to eat at one of the little-themed restaurants and food never tasted so good.

Edward hands me the ketchup and I groan as my weary limbs sink into the chair.

He raises his eyes and I shake my head. "Holidays are

exhausting. Are they always this busy?"

He laughs. "I doubt it. We have to pack everything in because we're here to do a job. I'd hope if I was here on holiday, I wouldn't be feeling like I needed one by the end of it."

I laugh softly. "Yes, we've certainly packed a lot in already. Will every day be this exhausting?"

He nods ruefully. "Unfortunately, Orlando is the home of everything fun and there is lots to do here. We have two activities a day to pack in and a ton of restaurants to check out. It's a place that many people aspire to visit at least once in their lives so we will be doing quite a feature on it."

I look at him with interest. "What do you get out of it?"

He grins. "We recommend a place and if they book as a result of clicking a link on our website, we earn a fee. It's free advertising for the hotels etc and if they get a good write up, they stand to gain many bookings. We also have links to all the attractions, restaurants and activities on offer and only include the ones we think would get the best results."

I stare at him with fascination. "I never knew, I just thought you wrote about it for a magazine. I never knew about this clicking thing."

He raises his eyes. "It's a very different world now, Amanda. Affiliate links drive sales and any business would be a fool to ignore their power. Most of our readers are now online and we have a mailing list of hundreds of thousands. That's alongside the subscribers to our YouTube channel and the likes on Facebook groups. Twitter also rakes in the subscribers and we are always looking for more channels to explore and grow our readership."

My mind struggles to take in this new information and I shake my head. "So, Saskia was right when she said she could have a career as a blogger. That's really what you are, isn't it?"

He laughs. "I suppose it is. Your daughter is quite correct. It's a different world we live in now Amanda. It moves at a startling pace and we have to run to keep up."

I roll my eyes. "So that's why it's so hard to keep up with you? You certainly travel at quite a pace."

Edward grins and for some reason, it stops me in my tracks. This new Edward is confusing me in a number of ways. Now I don't hate him anymore I have seen another side of him that is making me more interested than I should be. I no longer can't stand him but feel intrigued about the man I am on holiday/business with. He is human after all and seeing that hint of vulnerability in him earlier has made me see him in a new light. Maybe it's the mother in me that feels the need to care for him and reassure him that everything will be alright. The trouble is, it's the new sex addicted, out of control, harlot in me that is craving more than just friendship from this man.

Looking down, I try to distance myself from the feelings that have been growing all day. Edward Bastion is now consuming my thoughts and doing things to me inside that I have no business listening to. Poor man, if he knew about these new feelings, he would run a mile.

I am interrupted as Edward sighs heavily and says wearily, "Right then, time to join another line and endure yet another excruciating ride."

Laughing, I roll my eyes. "Don't be so cynical, Edward. Embrace your inner child and remember the magic. There's a lot more to this place than a commercial venture you know."

Shaking his head, he sets off at full speed again. "If you say so. I've yet to be convinced there's anything other than a licence to print money here, fuelled by the gullible holidaymakers who convince themselves this place is everything they ever dreamed of."

The day turns to night and the place lights up all around us. The castle is bathed in the ever-changing colours of the rainbow and the heat has turned to a lesser heat.

As we wait in yet another interminable line, I look around me in awe.

"This place is at its most magical at night. Look at the beautiful fairy lights and different colours stained on the building. I actually think I want to live here now. I wouldn't mind that house next door to the Christmas shop. I have visions of me skipping down Main street to do a stint at the ice cream parlour before tending to my rows in the Disney garden."

Edward laughs out loud and I see his eyes twinkling in the shadows. "You're one strange woman, Amanda Swallows. Did you ever grow up?"

I nod and feel a wave of sadness suddenly come over me. I'm not sure how it happened but yes, I did grow up. My childhood fascinations and dreams were replaced with more practical adult ones. The magic was replaced with real life and the dreams turned to dust in my eyes.

I see Edward staring at me with concern and I laugh self-consciously. "We all have to grow up, Edward. It's the journey of life. Though sometimes I wish I never had. Life was certainly simpler back in the day I never knew the pain of emotions just the physical ones."

He looks at me thoughtfully. "You sound as if you had a great childhood."

Smiling, I nod and my eyes mist over as I think of my parents. "Yes, I did. I was an only child and adored by my parents. They couldn't do enough for me and I suppose I was spoiled a great deal. We never had much money, but I felt like the richest kid in school. They made life fun and I tried to bring that to my own life with my children."

The line starts moving faster and Edward whispers as we walk. "What happened to your father? You speak of your mother but I don't think you've mentioned him."

The tears threaten to fall as I think about my lovely, good, kind, amazing father. Smiling brightly, I say ruefully, "He died of a heart attack when I was 15. It was very sudden, and we were in total shock for quite some time after. My Mum was devastated but makes sure she lives her life to the full now while she can. She's rarely home and seems to spend most of her time on one trip or another. In fact, she's probably one of your target consumers."

Edward smiles but I can see he is thinking hard.

Before we can continue, we reach the front of the line and take our seats in the little-painted boat that will ferry us around the little land of small people that sing their same tune for the duration.

As we set off Edward says wearily. "Kill me now and put me out of my misery."

Looking around, I see the excited faces of the children and the resigned ones of the adults and laugh. Nudging him I grin, "Come on, forget you're such an asshole for five minutes and see this ride through the eyes of a child."

He shakes his head as we sail off into the sunset, or should I say the pre-fabricated lands representing every nation in the world?

Ten minutes later and we're back out with the masses. Edward groans. "Forty minutes to queue for what must have been the most banal and tedious experience of my life. I think we should call this a day and head back for some much-needed rest."

I nod in agreement.

I'm right behind you. In fact, why on earth couldn't you have just looked around the place, gone on a few rides and then taken your pictures and leave. Is it really necessary to put yourself through endless hours of queues?

Even in the dusky light, I see an expression cross Edward's face that takes my breath away. His eyes soften and his mouth twitches and he looks at me with a genuine smile and says, "To be honest, we could have left hours ago. The reason we didn't was because you said you had always wanted to come here. I felt bad that your first experience abroad started off so badly. So, Amanda, I have kind of made it my mission to show you what you have been missing out on all these years. This holiday is your holiday and I'm your tour guide."

I just stare at him with utter amazement and can't actually form any words. He laughs and says quickly, "Come on, I think we need to get a good position to watch the parade from. We can only leave when the show has finished. Tour guide's orders."

Then he winks and grasps my elbow and propels me towards a clearing on the side of the little road where I notice staff setting up ropes for the parade. I think at this moment everything changes for me and Edward. I no longer hate the man; I think I love him. The trouble is, he must never find out.

CHAPTER 20

♪♪ *When you wish, upon a star*
Makes no difference who you are
Anything your heart desires will come...to...you.
Like a bolt out of the blue,
fate steps in and sees you through.
When you wish upon a star, your dreams...come...true ♪♪

The song starts in my dreams and ends up in my waking thoughts. The magic of Disney has followed me home and set up residence in my heart. A warm feeling spreads through me as I remember the magical evening Edward and I shared.

The parade was like nothing I had ever seen. Disney characters illuminated against the dark skies waving and coming to life before my eyes. I think I even shed a tear or two I was so emotional. But then came the light show followed by the fireworks. I was mesmerised. The whole of the Disney story came to life before my eyes and I could think of nothing else. I watched the amazing show and just stared before me in total awe. Whoever called it the Magic Kingdom wasn't joking. Even Edward cracked a rare smile and as we walked back to the car surrounded by the population of a small country, I felt happier than I have felt in years.

Suddenly my iPad makes that skypy noise and my anxieties come rushing back. What if it's the police with news of my mother's kidnap, or worse? What if they picked Ryan up for his man whoring ways and what if Saskia has found out that her mother is a fraud and a liar?

Quickly, I grab the window to my real life and hit the button. I am surprised to see Ryan's face fill the screen, and he looks at me a little strangely.

"Yo, mum. What's happening, are you ill?"

My relief at seeing his familiar face gives way to utter mortification as I realise I'm sitting in bed looking like a lush. My hair is all over the place and my face devoid of any make-up to pretend to the world that I'm actually younger than I really am.

Quickly, I improvise and croak, "Oh, sorry, honey, just feeling a little under the weather today."

He shrugs, seemingly not bothered.

"Can you put some money in my bank? I've run out and Dad's too busy with his honeymoon to give me any."

The blood rushes to my head as I try to think of a reason why I can't. Shaking my head sadly, I croak, "I wish I could, honey. The trouble is, the doctor's been and said I need total bedrest for 24 hours."

He looks annoyed and not at all concerned that his mother may be dying.

"What, can't you even get dressed and walk to the bank? That's ridiculous."

I shake my head ruefully. "I know, mad isn't it? The trouble is, up here in the… um… Lake District, there's an epidemic of um... beetle flu. Yes, I've been struck down and need to be quarantined for 24 hours. I'm sorry, honey, can you last until then?"

He sinks back on some sort of settee and looks irritated. "I'll have to. You know, you really should have stayed at home. It's not good that you're away as well."

I smile apologetically and then hate myself for not shouting at him, telling him what a selfish moron he is and to bloody well get out and earn his own money for a change and act like a man.

Images of him now as a man-whore spring to mind and I try to push them away before I am seriously freaked out.

I croak weakly, "So, it's good to see you, anyway. How was the wedding, did you meet anyone nice?"

I think I hold my breath as he reverts back to grunting his response. Other than when he wants something, conversation with Ryan is decidedly one-sided. He escapes my interrogation by a loud voice interrupting, "Is that mum? About time she answered the call of her children."

Ryan looks irritated and scowls as Saskia pushes him to one side and her angry face fills the small screen.

"Good god, mum, you look terrible. You're looking so old and withered. Have you been on the wine again?"

Ok, the magic of Disney is fading as fast as a snowman in the Florida sun. I shrug angrily.

"Thanks, darling. You really know how to make a girl feel good."

She rolls her eyes. "You haven't been a girl for a very long time. Anyway, listen. Dad and Lucy have taken off to Paris for a couple of days and left us with her family. Well, I'm not lying when I say they are seriously weird. I mean, they are so strict and it's like being in an episode of Prison Break. They have even forbidden me to be alone with Nicola. I mean, who are these people to dictate what I can and can't do? They are seriously messing with my future here and I need you to put your parental foot down and tell them to back off."

I feel quite faint as I see my offspring looking at me with annoyed faces and I start to cough weakly. "I'm sorry, darling. I'm not sure what you think I can do."

Saskia folds her arms and I know I'm in trouble.

"Listen, mum. Stop being so selfish and spending your free time in bed all day. I'll go and get Lucy's Aunt and Uncle and you can tell them that Ryan and me are allowed to see whoever we want, whenever we want. If we want to go to all-night parties like the other French kids do, then that's up to us not them. Oh, and while you're at it, please tell them that we are not required to eat absolutely everything on our plate including the frigging garnish. I mean, who eats parsley for god's sake? These people are mad, mother. I'm telling you they are out of control; certifiable buzzkills and we are in hell over here."

She shoves the iPad at Ryan and heads off to get the weird relatives. Ryan stares at me sulkily and I feel the screams starting in my head. I notice another call flashing for attention and feel some relief as I say, "Oh, sorry, honey, I have to go, someone else is coming through and it may be granny. You haven't heard from her at all by any chance, have you?"

Ryan says nothing and just closes the screen angrily. I feel my heart beating as I pray to the gods of Disney magic that it's my mother. Instead, I see Tina's anxious face filling the tiny screen.

"Oh my god, Amanda, did that man rough you up a bit after you called him all those things?"

Once again, I feel as low as a girl – sorry - old woman can get as I shake my head ruefully.

"No, I've just woken up after a very long day yesterday. I'm so worried though, Tina. I still haven't heard from my mum. It's not normal and something must be seriously wrong."

She looks concerned. "Maybe you should contact the police. I'm sure you can call them on one of those phone cards from America or email them or something."

The knot in my stomach won't lessen as it all comes flooding back.

Tina looks concerned. "You know I'm sure she's fine. Maybe they don't have a signal in Sardinia or she's forgotten her charger. Some people go off the radar when they're in a foreign country to detox or something."

I think about her words and realise it's just the sort of thing my mother would do. She's into all this alternative stuff and did spend some time in some sort of boot camp for relieving the stresses of coping with a modern life for the elderly.

I feel a little better and smile at Tina.

"You know, I think you're right. Anyway, how about you? How's Antigua?"

She grins and giggles like a teenager. "Fantastic. Derek and I have re-discovered our inner teenager and I'm not going to lie; this holiday has had more action than a week on one of Bear Grylls training expeditions."

I stick my fingers down my throat and pretend to gag. "Ugh, too much information."

She laughs. "How about you? Did you manage to rope in hot man and get him to satisfy all those wild sexual fantasises the HRT has spun in your head?"

I think I must go red because she gasps, "Oh my God,

Mandy Moo. You like him, don't you? I knew it. It was as certain as the night I lost my virginity in Croydon. Ugh, that didn't sound right, did it? Maybe we should have called our first-born Wallington or something else. Anyway, back to you and hot pants. You like him, don't you? Come on, tell me everything."

I groan and stick my flaming cheeks in my hands. "Stop it, Tina. You don't know anything. Edward is just being kind and showing me how to have a good time on holiday."

Tina snorts. "Is that what it's called these days? Well, enjoy away, honey because I want to hear all the juicy details when you get back."

Suddenly, she edges closer to the screen and whispers, "He's not in bed with you now, is he?"

I shriek, "Stop, no, of course not."

She looks hopeful. "In the shower then, cleaning off the results of a morning well spent."

I giggle and whisper loudly, "No, stop. I'm here on my own and he's probably in his room or on the balcony or something. You know, your imagination is way out of control. Are you sure you're not over indulging in the all-inclusive alcohol at this early hour?"

She grins. "I may have indulged in a little champagne for breakfast. It would be rude not to."

She winks and then blows me a kiss. "Anyway, got to go, we've booked a trip to the main town for some souvenir shopping. Have fun, babe and do everything your head tells you not to."

She closes her screen and I sink back against the pillows, suddenly a seething mass of anxiety.

What am I doing? I shouldn't be here thousands of miles away from my children when they obviously need me. My mother is missing, presumed dead – by me and my life is falling apart.

Then I think of Edward and my word rights itself. It doesn't matter - any of it. This is my week to rediscover myself and live the dream. This is my week to fulfil my fantasies and make my dreams come true. It's the law in Orlando. Wish upon a star and your dreams will come true. A small smile flits across my lips as I think about the wish I very much want to come true. How did hate turn to love in the blink of a vulnerable expression? It's time to ignore what my stupid head says and let my heart take over.

Placing the iPad firmly in the drawer, I spring from the bed like a gazelle. So what if I'm no longer a teenager? I'm a middle-aged woman of the world whose lessons in life are about to count for something. I know what I want and even if I don't get it, I can at least have fun pretending - can't I?

CHAPTER 21

After a hot shower and a serious make-up session, I breeze out of my room looking for Edward. Once again, he is tapping away on his iPad on the balcony and I head out to join him.

My heart beats a little faster as he looks up and smiles. Wow, Edward is certainly hot. Tina's right about that. Once again, he is unshaven and the sun from yesterday has deepened the tan on his face. His strong arms rest on the table and my mouth waters at the sight of his muscles straining against the thin fabric of his t-shirt. I can also see a smattering of a hairy chest as my eyes travel to the 'v' in his t-shirt. Before they travel down in search of another kind of 'v' I blink and smile brightly.

"Morning, Edward. That was quite a day yesterday, I'm exhausted."

He shakes his head. "Yes, I must be getting old because I'm still feeling it this morning."

Grabbing the chair opposite, I look at him with interest.

"So, what's happening today?"

He looks at his ever-present iPad and grins.

"An Air boat ride this morning, followed by a water park this afternoon."

I feel my face fall a little and he looks concerned.

"What's up, don't you like the sound of that?"

I look at him nervously. "Will there be crocodiles?"

Leaning back, he looks at me with a hint of amusement in his eyes and smirks. "Firstly, they don't have crocodiles here, they have alligators. Secondly, you won't be required to enter the water at all so will be perfectly safe. If it's any reassurance I've been on an airboat a few times and they are perfectly safe."

Shaking my head, I say softly. "I'm sure it will be perfectly lovely. What about the water park though? I'm not much of a swimmer."

He grins and rolls his eyes. "Then you'll be fine there too. Nobody swims at a water park. You just need to slide and ride. If it gets too much just go for a spin around the lazy river in a tube. They're quite a lot of fun, really."

Feeling a little better I look out over the lake and it strikes me how idyllic life here is in Florida. The sun always seems to shine and my problems seem a world away. The trouble is, thanks to technology they have followed me here and now I feel light years away from being able to deal with them and enjoy this holiday of a lifetime.

I hear Edward say softly. "Is everything ok, Amanda. You don't seem yourself this morning."

I shrug and say wearily. "I'm still worried about my mother. I just can't seem to shake the feeling that something's wrong. It's so unlike her not to message me back and even the children seem unhappy. It's strange being here and not being able to deal with everything as I would normally do."

Edward looks at his iPad and then says briskly, "I had an email from the moneypennies this morning. They are five hours in front of us and have tried to locate your mother."

I lean forward with interest as he shakes his head. "Apparently, they contacted the WI who put them in touch with your mother's group. The email that came back makes for interesting reading. Here, see what you make of this."

He pushes the iPad towards me and I swear he can hear my heart thumping as he looks at me with concern.

Squinting, I look at the screen and try to absorb the words in front of me.

Dear Sir

Thank you for your email regarding the organised trip to Sardinia. Unfortunately, I cannot divulge any information about any member in particular due to privacy laws. I will pass on your concerns to the group leader and ask that the member in question contact you immediately. I can, however, offer you reassurance that all of our trips are closely monitored and well organised. There have been no reports of anything other than our members having a jolly good time. Thank you for your email and have a lovely day.

Ingrid Stevenson
Chair of Surrey Hills WI

Sighing, I pass the iPad back to him. "Well, that says absolutely nothing."

He smiles reassuringly.

"Well, at least you know everything is going to plan. I'm sure there must be a simple explanation for it."

Trying to smile, I nod and say weakly. "Maybe I should grab some breakfast. Some food may help. I've never been able to function before my morning caffeine dose and a bowl of cereal."

I head back inside and make myself a coffee and some cereal. I decide to make one for Edward as well and it strikes me how strange this experience is. Here I am, thousands of miles from home making coffee for a super-hot man who is every fantasy I've ever had wrapped up in the most intriguing of packages. I wonder why he's still single? He must have loved his wife so much that nobody else will ever measure up to her memory. I wish someone had loved me like that. If that isn't true love, I don't know what is.

He smiles as I set the coffee in front of him and stretches back and looks around him with a smile.

"You know, Amanda, sometimes I really love my job."

Wishing I hadn't just put the largest mouthful of cereal in my mouth, I just nod trying to look poised and cool. He waves towards the impressive view.

"I've been to some amazing places in the world and some not so amazing ones. Sometimes they all merge into one and it's difficult to write something engaging about them. However, this week I'm feeling inspired. It's surprised me because I thought this would be the week from hell."

I grin. "It certainly started out that way. Tell me about your other trips. They sound intriguing and I want to hear every juicy detail about those women that plague you wherever you go."

Edward rolls his eyes and shivers.

"They are usually your typical bored housewives. Most of them are divorced and looking for their next meal ticket. They see a single man who could give them a life filled with travel and something sparks inside them. Most of my trips are spent fighting off their advances and trying to ignore the suggestive looks and blatant attempts at flirting with me to get me into bed. This trip is quite refreshing because it's obvious I'm the last man in the world you would think of that way. It's made me relax a little more and actually enjoy myself for a change."

I nod in agreement and plaster an expression on my face of someone who is everything he has described and more. Behind that look, however, is a woman that is everything he has just described in his other companions. Somewhere along the line hate has turned to lust and interest and I can't pretend that I haven't fantasised about joining him in that absolutely huge bed and re-enacting every scene from Fifty Shades - twice!

Disappointment joins anxiety and guilt and I wonder if I will make it through this week without needing some form of medication. I am a mess of worry, self-doubt and so much guilt I should be locked away for life with no parole. It all comes flooding back as I think of my children, miserable and penniless, miles from home with strangers ruining what should have been a happy trip. Their father has married another woman and it must have been so strange. I should be supporting them in what must be an extremely emotional time, not galli-vanting around theme parks and wrestling with alligators and lust for the hot man before me. I am a bad mother who fails in just about everything in life.

Edward looks at me with concern. "Are you ok?"

I nod bravely. "Oh, I'm fine. I actually can't wait to get started. I've never been on an airboat before. In fact, any boat come to think of it. Not even those swan ones they have in the local park. This should be quite the experience."

Edward shakes his head and grins. "You know, considering your age you've certainly led a sheltered life."

My face must fall quicker than a bungee jumper because he immediately looks contrite.

"I didn't mean that you are old or anything. I mean, I think I'm way older than you and you have been doing much more admirable things than me with your time, like raising two children for one."

I roll my eyes. "Two things actually. Anyway, just for the record, how old are you, Edward?"

He pulls a face. "I'll be 50 next year. Now you know why I'm so angry all the time."

My heart soars just a little and my inner goddess dances with considerable relief. "Gosh, you're so old, Edward. Us 47ers must seem like teenagers to you."

Laughing, he stands and nods towards the door.

"Well, we don't have a moment to lose then, do we? We need to fit in some living before it's too late."

I roll my eyes. "Speak for yourself, I'm just getting started. Women of my age are in their prime and ready to take on the world. I just wish I was this adventurous twenty years ago. I wonder how different my life would be now?"

Edward looks thoughtful. "Sometimes it's the lessons we learn along the way that shape our future. We need to learn hard lessons to move forward with no fear. Take you for instance. You are here in a foreign country with a man you had never met. I could be a murderer or anything but your sense of adventure and free spirit made you take a chance. It's my job to show you what you've been missing out on all those years and who knows when you return, your future may be a very different one?"

I follow him out and his words bounce around inside my head. I think this has changed my life. I can already see a whole new world than the one I was charted on. For the first time in a very long time, I feel excited. I always knew there was more out there. What I didn't know was that it was up to me to go and find it. Waiting for something to happen was a recipe for failure. I owe it to myself to seize the moment and take my life by two hands and mould it into something that counts.

The strange thing is that as I make my decision, a little piece of the guilt I always carry around with me falls away from the woman I became. Like a butterfly from a chrysalis, I can feel my wings beating, ready to take flight into a glorious future. This is now my time, and it begins this morning on an airboat in the Everglades. Now who would have thought that two weeks ago?

CHAPTER 22

As Edward drives, I admire my Instagram - sorry, Brandy's Instagram. I have managed to post several exciting photos via Wi-Fi at the resort. I thought up little comments that would intrigue my children and take great satisfaction in finding several new people have followed me.

Edward notices me poring over my feed – technical term – and grins. "You know, I could help you with that."

As I look up with interest he shrugs.

"I haven't got where I am today by not learning every trick on marketing on social media. First of all, you need to add hashtags to your comments."

I roll my eyes. "I know that, Edward. I'm not that bad."

Quickly, I add a few in while he contemplates the Sat Nav and look at him with satisfaction. "So, how far is this place?"

He turns down a dirt track and laughs. "Approximately two minutes."

I look out of the window in surprise. "But we only left an hour ago. I thought it was in the Everglades."

Edward grins. "That's just the name of it. It's a bit commercial really but will do the job. All we need are some photographs and a description and then we can link in some other ones to the article."

I nod and look with interest at the ramshackle shack tumbling down before us.

Everglades Airboat Safari

announces the business within and I feel a knot of nerves tying up my earlier bravery. This place looks like it would fail every health and safety inspection out there. Once again, I am about to trust my life to people who have obviously never heard of regulations and red tape.

Edward grins and pulls to a stop in the dust bowl of a carpark. "It'll be fine, trust me."

Now I'm very worried. For all his hotness he hasn't proved very reliable on the safety front so far. This could end in disaster.

I walk towards the shack with trepidation and note the peeling paint and the rusty ironwork littering the path. Even the door creaks open and the stale smell of a place that has no windows open greets us.

As I look around, I swallow hard and see alligator heads and photos of men wrestling the reptilian beasts on the walls. There are also various trophies on creaky shelves that could use a duster. There is a bar along one end and I see a wiley old man watching us approach through hooded eyes. I'm sure we must look a right pair of tourists. I am dressed in my white shorts with Saskia's Juicy Couture t-shirt and some huge black designer shades perched on my head. Edward's in khaki shorts with a white t-shirt carrying his usual camera bag over his shoulder.

I swallow hard and edge behind Edward as I wonder if we're about to be rustled out of here like strangers in Dodge. This place is everything I've ever imagined a wild west saloon to look like and I'm living the experience right here and now.

Edward says confidently. "We're here from Agora publications regarding the travel feature. I believe you're expecting us."

I see the man's eyes narrow and half expect him to draw his pistols and let us have it with both barrels. Instead, he just nods and smiles a brilliant white smile and says.

"Why didn't you say so? Welcome. I'm Grady and I'll be your guide today. Can I offer you a beer or a cold one before we get started?"

Edward shakes his head. "No, we're on a tight schedule so would be happy just to get started."

Grady nods and grabs some keys from the side and motions for us to follow him out.

We head towards the water's edge and I see an airboat waiting that I think looks ok. Compared to the bar this at least looks as if it was made this century.

Grady smiles and offers me his hand. "Here you go, darlin', jump on and I'll show you how the gators live."

Edward raises his eyes in a challenge as I very nearly wimp out. Shaking myself out of my fear I adopt my new Amazonian ways and step on board my first boat ever.

We sit on some high seats and I look at the swampyness around me with trepidation. The only thing keeping me from dwelling too much on the dangers all around us is the pressure of Edwards' leg next to mine.

Now that is all I can think of as Grady starts the

engine and we move away from the side. As the boat gains speed, I feel the wind whip through my hair and thank the god of new beginnings and twitter for bringing me here. Edward is pressed against me and it feels so good. He is obviously oblivious to the quivering mess beside him as he snaps away with his camera.

After my initial fear, I start to relax. Grady, for all his earlier strangeness, is actually a great tour guide. He points out various creatures and points to several suspect looking shapes loitering in the swampland. I am in awe of my surroundings. This is as close to nature as I think I have ever been and I've been to Chessington World of Adventures. It almost feels as if I am a million miles away from civilisation and all my troubles are left firmly behind me as I totally absorb this new experience.

I enjoy watching Edward at work and can't deny the pleasure he gives me as he points out various things of interest. I lean in shamelessly, pretending that I can't hear him over the noise. This is the most relaxed I've been since we arrived and as the sun beats down on my face, I push my worries aside and just enjoy the whole experience.

By the time we make it back to the car, I sense a shift in my relationship with Edward. He no longer appears to see me as a preying man-eater and it almost feels as if we are friends. I am kind of hoping that will develop into becoming friends with benefits but I'll take friends over enemies any day of the week.

I chatter excitedly about what we saw and scroll through my photos to select one for Instagram. I think I'm becoming as obsessed with my phone as my children. I never knew they could be so much fun. I mean, the pleasure I get when I see that someone I don't even know likes my picture makes me feel famous or something.

Edward drives us to a waterfront bar for lunch and I smile inside. I've made it. I am a perfect person for once in my life. I am living the dream. I have a sexy man beside me who goes out of his way to make sure I'm having a good time. We eat like the perfect people where money is of no consequence. I am even drinking wine in the afternoon and enjoying adult conversation for once. Tescos seems like a million miles away and Veg man ceases to hold any interest for me in this magical land. The worm is definitely turning and I like it – a lot.

After lunch we head back to the resort to change for the water park. I'm not going to lie; the thought of ogling Edward in his Speedos is doing strange things to me inside. The only trouble is the sight of me in my bikini may put him off me forever. I used to be stick thin as a teenager, much like Saskia is now. Then two children later and an obsession with Krispy Kreme doughnuts and a strange gym aversion, I'm no longer a size 10 and have acquired curves where they have no business being.

As I change, I sigh as I look in the mirror at the woman I am now with the eyes of the girl I once was. How did this happen? I need that girl back because with my new freedom I need to milk it for all its worth. My body can't get in the way of my rampant mind. Maybe I should give the gym another try. No pain no gain as they say and it's about time I took charge of my body rather than it taking charge of me.

I post a few pictures on Instagram while I can and look with interest at Saskia's page. As I see her familiar selfie pout, I sit on the bed and a huge wave of homesickness comes over me. How I miss my babies. They may annoy me most of the time but I have to have them near me. They irritate the hell out of me but I wouldn't change them for the world. I must be a terrible mother to abandon them in this way at the most testing stage of their lives.

I flick over to Ryan's page and see my little boy staring out at me from Cyberspace. He looks so handsome and I can see why he's so successful with the ladies. His photos aren't as polished as Saskia's and there are way fewer of them. Just a few shots of him and his mates having fun doing things that boys do. You know, football and cars. Where did his life go so wrong that he felt the need to become a man-whore?

I am interrupted by the usual skypy noise and rush towards it hopefully. I know it shouldn't but my heart sinks as I see it's from Robert. The anxiety hits me like a tidal wave as in two seconds flat I imagine the worst. He can only be calling me for one thing. Something's gone wrong and my children are involved.

I answer it quickly and as I see his incredulous expression; I realise just a little too late that I'm in my bikini in a strange bedroom. Why it should worry me, god only knows? I mean, he's seen more than I'm showing him before but all the same I quickly grab a pillow and almost shout, "It's not the kids, is it?"

He looks surprised and then shakes his head. "No, of course not, I'm sorry, they're fine."

The relief is overwhelming but is quickly replaced with irritation. "What is it then?"

He looks a little furtive and says almost hesitantly.

"Listen, I know it's my turn to have the kids and all. But it would be a huge help if you could have them for the rest of the week."

I just stare at him in amazement. "What?"

He carries on looking a little shady. "Well, as you know it's my honeymoon and they are kind of getting in the way."

I sit down heavily on the bed and stare at him in shock. He carries on.

"It's just the rest of the guests have left and now it's the four of us. I don't think it's fair on Lucy so I was going to pay for them to come home early. I think they would be happy because I sort of mentioned it already, and they seemed happy enough."

A million thoughts bounce around my brain as I struggle to form a coherent sentence. This is a disaster.

He inches a little closer to the screen and says in surprise, "Why are you wearing a bikini? I thought it was cold in the Lake District. Come to mention it, your face also looks a little red. What's going on, Amanda?"

I feel like a deer caught in headlights. I want to hit the screen with my pillow imagining it to be Robert's head connecting with a brick.

Then a bad situation turns decidedly worse as I hear a sharp knock on the door and Edward says loudly, "Are you ready, Amanda?"

Robert looks behind me in disbelief and stutters, "Who was that? Are you with - a man?"

His eyes narrow and the look on his face is absolutely priceless. I almost want to screenshot it and have it made into a canvas but I do the only thing any self-respecting coward would do in a situation like this. I snap the iPad shut and disconnect the call.

I quickly shout, "Sorry, coming."

In two seconds flat, I haul a t-shirt dress over my head, slide on the flip flops and grab my bag. I am going to pretend that call never happened.

I feel the anger clawing at me inside. How dare he.

How dare my cheating, wife abandoning husband put his new wife over his children? He invited them. He spends hardly any time with them and he is responsible for bursting their cosy little bubble of a life with two loving parents. He can just jolly well deal with them for a few more days because for once I am not going to bail him out. Let's see how his new wife deals with the stress of family life because like it or not, she is now step mum to two teenagers from hell.

CHAPTER 23

I now officially love water parks. Considering I'm a rubbish swimmer and have perfected the swim walk, I love the freedom of the rides in a water park. There is no swimming as you sit on a buoyancy aid careering down a water slide. No swimming required as you float around the lazy river supported by a rubber ring. And no swimming required as you cling onto your companion on the family ride.

However, most of all I love water parks because I get to stare at the body of a man with so much to give a hormonal woman. I almost drool at the sight of Edwards strong muscles rippling as he moves. The smattering of dark hair begs for me to rub my face in it and the tight swimming shorts draw my eye front and back throughout the whole afternoon. I think my eyes remain firmly lowered for the duration as my fantasy world goes into meltdown.

My earlier anger vanished like the ice creams we bought to cool off. Robert who? I am putting myself first for once in my life and far from feeling guilty about it; I feel empowered. The only thing spoiling my day is the worry I'm still feeling about the whereabouts of my mother.

I must go a little quiet because I see Edward looking at me with concern. "Are you ok, Amanda. You're not tired, are you?"

Shaking my head, I say sadly, "I'm still worried about my mother. She's in her seventies, not so you'd notice though. She is incredibly active and puts me to shame. But what if something's happened? It's not her age that bothers me. I would worry if Saskia or Ryan didn't reply to my messages too. I really do think something is terribly wrong."

Then something unbelievable happens. Edward looks at me with a soft look and reaches out and pulls me to him. He folds his arms around me and whispers, "It's ok, Amanda. Whatever it is, you're not on your own. I'm sure there'll be an email working its way to you to reassure you and put your mind at rest. Your mother will be having the best time ever and has probably just lost her phone or something. If it was more the WI email would have said so."

Shamelessly, I nestle in closer and almost forget what I'm worried about. Thoughts of my lost mother are pushed aside by stronger ones of desire, lust and a feeling that has long abandoned me. The feeling of somebody caring for me for a change. Someone reassuring me and taking my worries away. Someone who cares enough to want to comfort me in my hour of need and make it all better. This feeling left me a zillion years ago it seems but as it comes rushing back, I realise just how much I've missed it. Tears spring to my eyes as I try to hold everything together. I almost fold right here and now but common sense prevails and I just sniff and say in a small voice, "Thank you, Edward."

Before he can reply we hear a terse, "Disgusting. In front of children too. Some people just can't contain themselves in public."

Startled, I pull away and see the derisive stare of a woman herding a group of Summer camp kids past us. Some are taking photos and giggling like the schoolgirls they are and I look up at Edward in shock. He winks and grins as he pulls me away.

I think I'm in shock for the rest of the day. Edward hugged me. We were nearly naked in broad daylight and he hugged me without a care. I re-live the experience for the rest of the afternoon. His male scent of sweat mixed with that musky man smell lingers in my nostrils. The feel of his strong muscular arms holding me tenderly makes me weak with longing. The look in his eyes and the softness to his voice causes my heart to flutter and give me false hope of something actually happening with this man.

Suddenly, I am shy around him. My heart is telling me things that my head tells me otherwise. Warning sirens are ringing loud and clear as I see him telling me of those other women.

He was just being kind – *he wants you*. He's a friend – *I want more.* When this week is over, you'll never see him again – *He will propose*. Real life will get in the way and he'll move on to the next travel companion - *I love him*.

Gosh, it doesn't take much to make me fall in love. One kind word and gesture and I'm a mess. I really need a good dose of reality and to face up to my real life.

When I head back, I'll ring the kids.

Edward appears totally unaware of my feelings for

him. He just chats about his work and tells me stories of all the places he's visited. I feign interest but my mind is out of control. I just can't push those feelings away of how it felt to be in his arms. It was almost worth my mother disappearing to give me the experience.

As soon as we reach the apartment Edward smiles with relief.

"Well, another full-on day. How about we get cleaned up and go for a nice meal somewhere local? I know just the place."

I smile with relief. "Great, it sounds just what I need. How long have I got?"

He consults his watch and raises his eyes. "Is one hour ok? I've got to write up today's events and then shower."

Nodding gratefully, I head toward my room and the impending showdown with my children.

For the first time since I arrived, I actually call them. As I listen to the weird noise telling them of my call, I feel the nerves tangling up inside me. The screen bursts into life and I see Saskia looking at me with something bordering on irritation/vulnerability. I think I hold my breath as she says in a strangely quiet voice. "Oh, hi."

Now I'm worried. Something is terribly wrong.

Immediately I say, "What's the matter, has something happened?"

I watch helplessly as the tears well up in her eyes and she sniffs. "It's fine. You know, it's hard being here with Ryan and Dad. Lucy's not you and I can't talk to her."

I put on my best motherly voice and say softly. "Tell me what's bothering you."

She looks at me through water-filled eyes and sniffs. "It's Nicola. I've suddenly realised I will have to leave soon and what we have will be gone in a flash. Long distance romances never work and as soon as I discover my soul mate, they are cruelly taken from me."

Still feeling strangely disturbed by the whole conversation, I smile reassuringly. "It's not so bad. I'm sure you'll keep in touch. There's always the Eurotunnel and flights are so cheap these days, I wouldn't worry about it."

She sniffs. "Why did you have to go to the Lake District? It's weird thinking of you there and not at home where you belong."

I smile sympathetically but there's that small part of me that wishes my children would see me as a person with hopes and dreams just like them. It's as if you give up any sort of claim to a life of your own when they arrive. They can't seem to comprehend that you would ever want anything other than to be at their beck and call all the time. Not once have they asked me how I am given that my husband has just married someone else. They haven't asked me about my holiday and don't appear in the least bit interested in how I'm filling my time. They just seemed annoyed when I was ill as if it was an inconvenience to them.

Sadly, I wonder where I went wrong. Was I ever like that? I can't remember being like it but then again, maybe I was.

Saskia peers into the screen. "You know, mum, you must remember to wear make-up at all times at your age. If anything, it acts as a barrier to the elements and if I'm honest your complexion is looking a little ruddy. Nobody wants to be old before their time and I don't want an ageing mother in my wedding photos. Remember to do your make-up as I showed you and you won't go far wrong."

She smiles as if she has just given me a pot of gold of

wisdom and I try to shake off the fact that I want to scream at her. Instead, I try to find out more about her brother.

"So, tell me how's Ryan bearing up?"

She shrugs looking bored already.

"Who knows? I mean, you know him. His head's so far inside his video games I'm not sure if he even registers normal life anymore. He's so lucky though. He only has to look at a girl and they beg for his Snapchat. Why is life so unfair? I work so hard at getting noticed and all he does is look at someone and Wham Bam thank you, mam."

If I wasn't already sitting, I think I'd pass out. Wham Bam, no surely not, not Ryan.

I'm almost afraid to ask but must know.

"So, um… is he still seeing anyone in particular?"

She shakes her head angrily. "He'll be lucky. Not only were we chained to the strictest couple of buzzkills in the world while dad and Lucy took off with no regard for our feelings but then all the other guests left leaving us with only the chickens to entertain us. Ryan's in a foul mood – no pun intended – and can't even get online to play his games because the signal's from the seventies over here. This place is seriously behind the times and doesn't even have a dishwasher. We are expected to make our own beds and help with the chores. I mean, chores! I ask you, who asks their kids to do chores these days? No, I'm telling you, mum, if it wasn't for the fact there is a channel of water separating us from the green fields of home, Ryan and I would have escaped this hellish prison and hitch-hiked home quicker than you can say au revoir. That's French for goodbye if you didn't know."

Feeling a flash of irritation, I snap. "Of course, I knew

that. I did have an education you know before I enrolled in the workhouse, otherwise known as marriage."

She shrugs. "Anyway, it's good you called because I want you to tell daddy and Lucy that I want to go to college here next year. Nicola says the local one's amazing and there are all sorts of great parties and the like. Life is like an American film out here and makes my school look like something from the dark ages."

I'm not sure what to say to any of this, really. College in France? My daughters delusional if she thinks that's an option now Brexit has been triggered. So, I say what any normal stressed mother of teenagers would say in this situation and smile softly. "Ask your father, darling. I'm sure he'll be able to sort something out."

Saskia groans. "I already have. He told me 'no' with no arguments. He said that if I even passed my GCSEs, which he said was highly doubtful as to pass them people needed to actually put in some work and revise. I mean, how rude. He doesn't even live with us. How does he know I'm not a slave to my books? No, I'm telling you, mum, things are bad out here and you're no help at all. We're in crisis and all you seem to do is laze around in some kind of bedroom all day and appear to have really let yourself go."

Counting to ten in my mind, I shake my head and put on a stern face. "Listen, darling. It's only for a few more days and then you'll be home. It's not fair of you to upset things, it is your father's honeymoon after all. Why can't you just smile and grit your teeth and pretend to be enjoying yourself? It's not as if you spend much time with him as it is, so you should make this time count for something. Try to get to know Lucy a little and you may discover you have shared interests. Sometimes you just have to put others before yourself and this is one of those times."

She looks at me as if I've grown two heads or something and snaps. "It's ok for you enjoying '*me*' time and doing whatever you want. No, as soon as I can I'm leaving home and setting up home on my own. Then I can do whatever I want without anyone bringing me down. I mean it, mother, I'm not joking. All of this abandonment will come back to bite you one day."

Before I can reply I see her look up and scowl. "Oh, Ryan wants a word."

Feeling a surge of relief, I smile as my son's face fills the small screen.

"Hey, mum. You got to the bank yet?"

Trying to ignore my head screaming at him like the mad woman I am inside, I just shake my head. "No, I'm sorry there isn't a bank for miles."

Well, I'm not lying. Probably 5000 miles to be exact.

He looks at me angrily. "Haven't you ever heard of telephone banking? Normal people do things online these days. You could have done it by now without leaving your bedroom."

Like a deer caught in headlights, I try to think of a response and just say weakly, "I've never trusted computers with my personal details. You can't beat good old-fashioned face-to-face banking with a human, not a machine. I could be targeted by Cyber thieves and then we would have nothing."

I watch as they share a look of resignation. Saskia rolls her eyes, "God, I can't believe we actually made it this far with you two as parents. Mum, you really should drag yourself into this century. Even I know the banks will pay you back if you get robbed on the superhighway. You really are sooo old sometimes."

Ryan just looks angry – as usual and heads off without so much as a 'goodbye mummy I love you.' My heart sinks as I try to remember when he last looked at me with any other expression than anger. I sigh and say to Saskia, "Is he ok? He looks unhappy."

She shrugs. "He appears to be fixated on someone we both follow on Instagram called Brandy and is trying to cyberstalk her to get her contact details. I mean, who obsesses over someone who lives in an iCloud? You really should have words with him you know, it's not as if Brandy would ever be interested in someone like him, anyway."

What?! I can't believe this is happening. I feel ill. My son is obsessing over a girl who is actually his mother. Now I know things are messed up.

Suddenly her eyes spark with excitement and she leans forward. "You know, mum, Brandy is living the life I dream of. She's a super blogger. You know, what I was telling you about. You should see her pictures. She's even met Cinderella. Yes, I know, cool isn't it? I really think I'll apply to become a Disney Princess. It must be the best job in the world. Oh, and she's posting these great photos of what she's up to and Ryan thinks she's his soulmate because she appears to be into everything he is."

She rolls her eyes. "As if someone like that would be interested in a douche like him. No, I expect she hangs out with other bloggers in some sort of blog club for the elite. You know, I bet she knows Zoella. I expect they are best friends and everything and get invited to holiday for free in return for a mention on the blog. It just makes me all the more determined to follow in their footsteps. Who needs GCSEs when you can live the dream like they do. You don't need a qualification to post a picture and dad's living in the past if he thinks you do."

I hear someone calling her and she looks irritated. "Great, now we have to go and visit some gun factory over here tomorrow. I bet there are no frigging gun factories in the Lake District. I bet all you're doing is pigging out on cream teas and reading magazines. It's not fair, mum. Why did you and dad have to split up in the first place? Did our feelings come into it at all? Your generation is so selfish thinking of themselves all the time. When you have children, you are supposed to put them first not drag them behind your latest crazy scheme and expect them to grow up and actually want to be around you."

She shakes her head as if she's some sort of wise old owl and looks at me with pity. "Anyway, if I were you I'd probably go in search of the spa where you can detox and try to lose a few of the pounds that appear to have piled on during your trip away. Nobody wants a mother who's let themselves go. Remember, it's not just you it affects. Your children need a mother who looks semi-presentable in their online photo feed."

I'm actually not sure what to say as she looks away and shouts angrily, "All right, for God's sake I'm talking to my mother you know. Can't I even do that now?"

She turns to look at me and something about the sudden vulnerable look in her eyes makes me go cold. She blinks back the tears and sighs heavily. "Bye mum. Speak to you later."

Then she is gone, leaving me even more worried than when I first called. Why am I suddenly feeling like the lousiest mother alive?

CHAPTER 24

Taking extra care, I get ready for an evening out with Edward. Despite my anxiety about life back home I can't ignore my inner self begging to be noticed by a hot man. So, as Saskia requested, I make up my face exactly as she showed me and style my hair as it was intended to be worn when I had it cut. I'm also pleased to see the hint of a tan bringing me a healthy glow and overall feel quite satisfied with the results.

I decide to wear one of the charity shop borrows and pull on a Chloe dress that makes me feel like a million dollars. Maybe I'll buy this one after all. Surely every woman deserves a piece like this in her wardrobe. It shouldn't be too expensive because it is second hand after all.

After a splash of perfume, I am feeling much better. As I head out to find Edward things almost seem normal.

My heart beats a little faster as I see him waiting for me. He looks amazing in chinos and a smart white shirt. His tan is much deeper than mine and I can smell his distinctive aftershave from here. My heart flutters as he watches me approach with a blank face. This man is unreadable. I can never tell what he's thinking and for all I know he is counting down the days to get shot of me.

He smiles and then looks at me with a concerned expression. Suddenly, I feel nervous. What does that look mean? Do I look like an old person trying to look young? Is my dress transparent in the sun's rays and he can see my hold it all in passion killer underwear through the sheer fabric? Is my make-up smudged or is my perfume making him feel sick? My anxiety is now off the scale as he smiles and nods towards the chair next to him.

"Sit down Amanda, I've had an email from the moneypennies.

Ok, now my heart is beating like a drummer at a rock concert. There's something about the look in his eyes that tells me I'm not going to like what he's about to tell me."

I sit down and try to look unconcerned but I know my expression must be giving me away because he smiles softly.

"It's ok, I think?"

What does that mean? I think what?

He flips open his iPad and searches for the email. Then he pushes the computer into my hands and says gently.

"Here's the email I received. I'm sure it's fine."

As I take the device from his hands, I feel my heart hammering with trepidation. Am I ready to discover the fate of my mother? Will I crumble in front of the object of my heart's desire and put him off me forever?

With a deep breath I try to focus on the words on the screen and then frantically scan the neatly typed lines that may cause my world to implode in 3 seconds flat.

Hi Edward

. . .

We hope that things are progressing well in Orlando. Regarding the mission you set us we have had some intel that we need to share with you.

I look up as Edward laughs softly and rolls his eyes.

"I think they take their nickname a little too seriously sometimes."

I glance back to the words on the screen and read on with trepidation.

We had another email this morning which you will find under this one. I have checked with the hospitals and local police and there have been no reports of any sightings or hospitalisations. As soon as we get any more news, we will inform you immediately.

My heart races even faster if that's at all possible as I see another email from somebody called Sandra Dawson.

Dear Madam.

I understand you have concerns about an organised trip to Sardinia by the Surrey Fringe of the WI.

I felt obligated to inform you of what I know, as the official story is to pretend its business as usual. However, I cannot live with my conscience if I don't inform you of the extremely irregular activities unfolding in that distant land.

It appears that a breakout group of five members have left the safety of the Surrey group and indulged in an unsolicited and frowned upon merger with a group of sailors from Bristol.

The member in question, Dorothy Swallows has taken off with four other members to stay as invited guests on the super yacht of a businessman from the pre-mentioned county and acted against protocol and abandoned the organised activity schedule. They left two days ago and no contact has been forthcoming. Rest-assured we are doing our utmost to locate our members and have drafted in the local police. However, due to the fact they left voluntarily there is nothing more we can do. We are due to leave in three days' time so are hopeful for a safe return. I will of course keep you up to date with developments.

Please do not quote me or refer to this email in any way as I will be forced to deny any knowledge of going against protocol and notifying you of my concerns.

Anon

EDWARD LAUGHS. "Do you think she knows her name is showing alongside her email address?"

I shake my head as the worry gnaws away at me inside. Looking at him in horror, I stutter, "Do you think she's ok? You hear of all sorts of things happening to lone women abroad. What if they are being held captive and being used as sex slaves?"

Edward snorts as I try to ignore the voice inside my head berating me for not going on holiday with my mother after all.

"I think they'll be perfectly safe. They will be having an amazing time and it would explain the lack of communications. Maybe she doesn't want to tell you, or her battery is dead. I wouldn't worry, Amanda. Your mother is a grown woman and could probably teach both of us a thing or two about living life to the full. Just be happy for her and imagine she's having the time of her life."

I groan and put my head in my hands. "That's what I'm worrying about."

Inside I am stricken with worry for my children and now my mother. It's not fair. Why am I the only member of my family not having sexy fun this week? Typical of my luck. Stuck in the friend's zone while absolutely everybody else in the universe is indulging in illicit pursuits.

Edward takes the iPad from my hand and smiles. "Come on. There's nothing you can do so we may as well head out for a good meal. I know of a great little steak house not far away and you can drown your worries in a bottle of red wine."

I smile and follow him outside but inside I am a mass of contradictions and anxiety. I knew I should have never tried to find some *'me'* time. This week is all my fault for daring to want more and throwing caution to the wind. This is what happens when you veer off left in life. It alters the balance and life goes crazy. This is all my fault and now I'm going to have to live with the guilt forever.

CHAPTER 25

*E*dward and I are shown to a booth in the Little Rock Steakhouse. I look around in awe at the High Chaparral themed restaurant. This feels as if real cowboys live here and I look around in the hope of seeing a lusty one gazing at me with naked intent, spinning his lasso to rope me in. Instead, a server comes and shows us to our booth before thrusting a heavily laminated menu at us.

Edward looks around him with satisfaction and grins. "I'm looking forward to this. After the day we've had a huge steak is definitely on my wish list."

I smile and look at the menu wishing I could actually see it. The light is so dim in here and the words are just a blur in front of my eyes. Surreptitiously I peer closer and then try to hold it a little further away. I knew I should have kept that eye appointment. It's only because I hate that little puff of air that they torture you with that kept me away. I do have some off-the-shelf glasses from Poundland but I don't want Edward to see me in them. I can't spoil the illusion of youthful vitality just to satisfy my growling stomach.

By the time the server comes to take our order I've decided to wing it.

Edward nods and says, "Ladies first."

Pretending to be undecided, I say quickly, "Oh it's ok. You go first it'll give me more time."

I listen carefully while pretending to study the menu as he orders steak and fries with a side of corn.

Marissa, our amenable server turns to me.

"How about you, honey?"

I just wave the menu in the air and say matter-of-factly. "Oh. That sounds good. I'll have the same."

She smiles and takes our menus and heads off leaving me to breathe a sigh of relief and pat myself on the back for a crisis of age diverted.

Edward smiles and leans forward. "So, tell me. How is Brandy doing on the super highway?"

I laugh and then picture Ryan stalking my alter ego and the anxiety comes flooding back. I stutter. "Things are a bit weird regarding Brandy."

Edward looks interested. "In what way?"

I groan. "I've done such a good job in appealing to my children's interests that my daughter now wants to copy my every move and is even more determined to become a professional blogger. That isn't the worst thing though. It appears that I am Ryan's idea of a dream girl and could very well be his soulmate. He is currently cyberstalking Brandy in the hope of tracking her down, probably to unleash his man-whoring ways on her."

I have to laugh at the shock on Edward's face as he says, "Come again. I think you should start at the beginning."

I quickly take an absolutely huge gulp of wine.

MORE FROM LIFE

"The trouble is, my children are becoming strangers to me. I thought I knew their every thought and wish and now I am floundering in an unknown world. Ryan is always locked in a virtual world and barely grunts at me. Saskia's informed me that he's become a man-whore and I tell you Edward, at absolutely no point when I held my baby in my arms did I look at him and say 'I hope you grow up to become a man-whore one day'. I have done such a good job at appealing to his interests on Instagram that he now believes 'Brandy' is his soul mate and is, as we speak, trying to Cyber stalk her location to unleash his whoring ways on her. Saskia, meanwhile, thinks life's all about the latest perfume or fashion brand. She is so desperate to have her first kiss that it appears that sex didn't matter. Her coveted first kiss occurred miles away from home with a girl called Nicola. Well, I can tell you, Edward, I never saw that one coming and I don't have a freaking clue how to deal with this."

Edward almost spits out his wine as he laughs loudly. I look at him with utter incredulity and say crossly, "I'm glad you're finding all of this so funny. I can assure you I do not."

He grins and says gently. "Did Saskia tell you Nicola was a woman?"

Nodding, I roll my eyes. "Well, of course she did. I mean, surely the name gives it away. For goodness sake Edward are you always this obtuse?"

He laughs again which really gets my back up and then says softly.

"Amanda, Nicola is a boy's name in France. A bit like Nicholas over here."

I just stare at him in utter amazement and try to ignore the feeling of pure and utter relief flooding through my whole body. Immediately I am annoyed with myself for not being all-encompassing and up with the times because I say in an annoyed voice.

"Well, I for one hope you are wrong. There's nothing wrong with being gay these days, Edward. It wouldn't have bothered me in the slightest. In fact, I have always prided myself on my liberal thinking and acceptance of all types of men and women."

Edwards eyes twinkle which stops me in my tracks. I can't tear my eyes away and words fail me as everything else fades into the background. I find myself having to push down a sudden desire to launch myself across the table like a shuttle at Cape Canaveral. He holds my eyes for just a fraction before we are rudely interrupted by Marissa who bangs a plate of bread and salad down on the table and thrusts serviette covered cutlery in our faces.

The moment is broken and I fall on the bread like a woman desperate to distract herself from her own wanton mind. Wow, Edward is so sexy it hurts. I must get a grip before he files me away with the other lustful women who he hates and abhors.

The bread is probably the best thing I have ever tasted and that from a Krispy Kreme addict. I find myself gorging on the manna from heaven as Edward smiles. "Carry on, I haven't had this much fun in years."

Shaking my head, I roll my eyes. "Then you don't get out much."

He looks so sad it takes my breath away. He looks at me through weary eyes and says sadly, "You're right. Ever since Karen died, I've just gone through the motions. It's been five years next month and the thought of starting again with someone else is too distressing to think about. It feels as if I would be disloyal to her

MORE FROM LIFE

memory if I met someone and carried on as if she had never been there. It's almost as if the memory of her will fade if I let another woman into my life."

His words pierce my heart and I feel such sympathy for him. He smiles sadly. "When Karen died a large part of me also died that day. She was my rock and my reason for living. Without her my life was meaningless. It was the hardest thing I have ever had to go through and the most painful. I have tried to date other women but just spent the whole time comparing them to her. They never measured up, and I ended up hating myself for trying. So, I became the angry man you had the misfortune to be saddled with on your first trip abroad. I'm sorry, Amanda. You didn't deserve to be lumbered with me; you deserve better."

My heart aches for him. He is lost and drowning in life with no reason to live. I smile at him softly. "You're wrong, Edward. You have so much to give a woman who deserves it. You are kind and caring and have made this trip one I will never forget for a number of reasons."

I pull a face and he laughs – a little.

"Edward, you will find happiness again. Karen wouldn't want you to turn your back on living the life you deserve. She loved you and would want the best for you. You will never forget her. She is a huge part of you and will live in your heart forever. The love you shared will never fade and grow cold in the realities of life. She will always be young in your mind and her smile will fill your dreams. You won't have to watch her fall ill or see her watching you suffer in life. The memories you have are pure and untarnished. Nothing will ever take them away and you must move on with your life and live it as she would want you to."

I can tell that my words have hit the spot because I

see the emotion in Edward's eyes as he takes a sip of his drink.

Then he fixes me with a look that alters everything for me as he says huskily, "Thank you, Amanda. Thank you for putting up with me and thank you for being you. But most of all, thank you for not being one of those dreadful women that I feared you were when I saw you at the airport. If I had to come away with anyone in the world and had a choice, I would have chosen you."

Luckily, the steaks arrive before I dissolve into a blubbering heap. Wow what just happened? Once again things have shifted with Edward and me. Now I know I'm in trouble because with every word spoken and every look or gesture I am falling completely and painfully in love with the angriest man I have ever met. The trouble is, if he knew he would hate me for it.

CHAPTER 26

Somehow, I get through the meal with my dignity intact. Edward fascinates me and I spent most of it asking him about his business and the places he's visited. It's all a world away from normal everyday life and makes my tales of life at Tescos seem completely mundane and boring. However, Edward appears fascinated with my stories of dealing with two teenagers from hell and an out-of-control senior. After describing one crazier escapade involving my mother I probe a little further into his life.

"Do you have a family, Edward?"

He nods and smiles. "Yes, my family live in Cheshire where I grew up. I don't see them as much as I'd like, but it's always good when I do."

I lean forward with interest. Finally, I can discover more about my enigmatic travel companion.

"I bet they're so proud of you."

He nods. "I think so. My father was a solicitor and my mother a doctor. I think they always hoped I'd follow them in a professional career and didn't understand my career choice in the slightest."

I say wearily, "I totally understand their confusion. When Saskia opens her mouth, a foreign language comes out. I just wish that Ryan did open his mouth and then wish he didn't half the time. I totally get your parents confusion. Maybe it's the law that we don't understand the world our children live in. It appears that you can't enforce your own upbringing on your children because life has moved on since you were their age. Things develop at a rapid pace and we are so intent on living in the past that when we catch up, we don't understand how we got there. Maybe I should just relax and let life take its course. I mean, what's wrong with blogging as a way to make money? I should encourage Saskia and try to understand this Cyber world she lives in, instead of judging her and forcing my own outdated wishes onto her. I'm not even sure what Ryan wants to do such is the level of communication we now share."

Edward looks at me sympathetically.

"It must be hard trying to deal with it on your own. Say no if you want to but what happened with your husband?"

Shrugging, I stare at him sadly. "We grew apart and travelled down different roads. He hated what I liked, and it was the same for me. Thinking back, we should never have married in the first place. Unlike you, I never had that soul mate thing. You're lucky you did, really. At least the memories keep you warm and mean something. Robert and I were good friends and it should have just stayed that way. Even now I wish him well and am happy for him finding Lucy. I've never had the all-out romance that I read about. In some ways, I'm glad of it because at least I don't know what I've been missing out on. No, my

MORE FROM LIFE

future is set. Join the management programme at Tescos as soon as I get back and try to be a good mother to my children. Then when they provide me with grandchildren, I can try to be a better one than I was a mother."

Edward frowns and I look at him in surprise. "What?"

He shakes his head and leans back in his seat.

"Honestly, Amanda I thought you were better than that."

I look at him with shock as he says angrily. "You are a fantastic mother and shouldn't forget that. You have done nothing but worry about your children since you got here and all you've done is try to do something for yourself for a change. Even I can see you are trying hard to understand their world, Brandy is evidence of that. You really should have more faith in yourself. Your kids will learn a lot more if their mother is true to herself. They will be proud if you allow your wings to unfold and fly as high as you can go. Don't settle for the ordinary in life. You only get one shot at it so make it count. Make every second count and don't let the sun set on a day without having tried to make it better in some way. This world you live in now has endless possibilities for someone like you and you should approach it with a clear head and a quest for adventure. When you land back at Gatwick, I want you to walk off that plane with a new spring in your step and a mind open to new beginnings. It's about time you started living before you can't anymore."

Wow! I'm actually speechless. Who saw that coming? Edward has floored me with that little speech and strangely it brings tears to my eyes. Nobody has ever thought I could do more than be a wife and mother. Nobody ever pushed me to seek more from life than what was expected and nobody ever looked at me with a mixture of disappointment, hope and something else that my brain can't file away as an emotion. This is one complicated man sitting before me and I'm not sure what to say now.

Luckily, I don't have to because Marissa brings us the dessert menu and once again, I must make my choice in life through blurred lines. Maybe one day those lines will sharpen. Maybe one day it will be clearer what to choose and I'll see clearly what has remained out of focus. Edward's right. Now is the time for new beginnings and the only person who can change my future is me.

When we leave the restaurant, I feel different. I walked in here one person and something happened to alter my mindset and the person who leaves sees things very differently.

We drive back to the hotel in a companionable silence and I mull over Edward's words. For the first time in many years I feel a tingle of expectation. I knew this week would change my life – how exactly is still resting among those blurred lines and out of focus. But it's there, which is the first step to discovering what it actually is. I need to open my eyes and look at the opportunities all around me. I knew this trip would change my life, this is it, new beginnings and a new me.

CHAPTER 27

When I wake the next morning, it takes a little time before the feeling hits me. This is it, my new beginnings day. Then why do I feel so exhausted and way older than my years? This isn't how I should feel – surely?

Once I'm ready, I head out to find Edward tapping away on his iPad as usual. He smiles. "Hey, did you sleep well?"

Sitting opposite, I groan. "Too well. I'm feeling a little jaded today if I'm honest. I suppose it's all caught up with me and my body is rebelling against the new super-me."

Edward laughs and leans back, fixing me with an amused stare that makes his eyes twinkle and raises him even higher in the demi-god status I have now applied to him.

"Well then, maybe today would be a good day to test out the facilities here. I think we deserve a morning of R&R and you can grab some sun and recharge your batteries.

Ok, now I do think I love this man. I think the relief must show because he laughs softly. "Do what makes you happy Amanda, remember the plan."

I laugh. "Well, what would make me the happiest is a large shot of caffeine. Do you fancy a coffee? I'll head over and grab one at the little shop if you like. If you're lucky, I may even throw in a Krispy Kreme doughnut."

He nods. "Great, thanks. There's some money in my wallet on the side. Take it from there and grab a receipt. Like I said, it's all expenses paid on this trip."

He turns back to his iPad and I head into the little apartment. Spying his wallet on the side, I feel like a thief as I remove a ten-dollar bill. As I do, I see a photograph nestling in the little plastic window and my breath catches as I see the beautiful woman staring back at me. Her smile is captivating as she stares at the camera with so much love and happiness. This woman is stunning. She looks confident and as if she has everything in life. Her smile is infectious and I find myself smiling as I look at her. Edward's right, life is so unfair. How can fate be so cruel as to take someone like that from a lifetime of shared hopes and dreams? It doesn't make sense and I totally understand Edward's anger.

I carefully close the wallet and start walking. Thoughts of Karen walk with me and I picture their perfect life together. Edward and Karen – super couple. Living the dream and making the most out of the life they were given. My heart aches for the woman who lost it all in the blink of an eye. Then my heart aches for the man left behind and the way his life also changed that day. Then my heart aches for the fact that I have never even experienced one second of the life they obviously shared. They are richer than me because of it. At least they had it for even a fleeting moment. I am still looking and had actually resigned myself to never finding it. Now however, I have changed and am recognising that life doesn't reach an age where it stops and you accept what it throws at you. I'm realising that to survive in this world you need to embrace change and move with it. I will find that special someone if it takes me the rest of my life to find him. However, it won't be my main focus because I am fast realising that I need to find the girl I once was before I can truly be happy.

Once I have purchased the coffee and doughnuts, I head back to the room. As I walk, I appreciate the beauty of the surrounding place. This is so far removed from my life it doesn't fail to knock me out every time I remember I'm actually here. Florida even smells different. It smells of hope and dreams and a life untainted with reality. It offers a world of excitement wrapped up in heart-warming sunshine. Once again, I wish the children were with me. I want them to share in this magical land and feel such a failure that I was never able to provide it.

I get back to the apartment and Edward looks up and smiles. "Perfect timing. I've written the article on yesterday and now we can concentrate on today."

Handing him the coffee I smile with interest.

"So, what's the plan?"

"We'll take advantage of the facilities here and maybe head out to the next main attraction in Florida this afternoon."

"Which is?"

He rolls his eyes. "The outlet malls."

Just when I didn't think this place could get any better Edward said the magic words. 'Outlet malls!' Surely every woman's dream and firmly number one on her bucket list. Wow, shopping in bargain heaven. I wonder if my credit card will withstand the onslaught it's about to receive. Will it set off alarm bells at the bank and cause the Cyber police to scramble? Ooh, I haven't been this excited since I discovered I was coming here in the first place.

Edward laughs. "I can see you're happy with the itinerary."

Grinning, I just shrug. "Whatever. Now if you'll excuse me, I need to prepare myself for a morning spent with the sun. I'll be in my room erecting the barriers to its harmful rays."

Edward smiles and as I head off, he suddenly calls out, "Oh, I nearly forgot. You've had another email."

Why is it that the new me is suddenly beaten to the ground by the old me racing back with a vengeance? The old anxious me looks at Edward with the fear of what is coming next.

Smiling reassuringly, he hands me the iPad and says, "Don't look so worried. Not every email signifies bad news. I'm sure your mum is having a whale of a time."

Nodding, I try to look as if I'm not the super-anxious out of control hormonal woman that I am and smile.

Looking down I read with trepidation.

Hi Edward

I hope life is good in the sunshine state. Just an update on the mission. We ran some background checks and discovered the Jolly Rogers are a group of fishing enthusiasts from Bristol. This is their annual expedition to discover marine life in different countries. The crew consists of five men of mature years who are well-respected in their local communities. I hope this puts Amanda's mind at rest. There has still been no word on the missing members but they are due to catch their flight home tomorrow, so we will know more then.

Thanks for the update on the Airboat ride. I have downloaded it to the relevant files for editing on your return.

Have fun

Moneypennies

THE JOLLY ROGERS! Edward laughs as he removes the iPad from my hands.

"Sounds pretty harmless. You've got to admire them though. I hope I'm still travelling the world in my seventies and taking advantage of what's on offer."

Groaning, I sink down onto the chair. "That's what I'm afraid of. The trouble with my mother is she has no filter. She doesn't think about what may go wrong just about what she wants at the time."

Edward grins. "Sounds as if I'd like your mother."

Shaking my head, I smile. "You would. The trouble is, I sometimes think I have three teenagers to worry about. She is worse than any of us and now I have to worry about her sailing on the ocean with a group of jolly sailors and just hope there's no rogering involved."

As soon as the words leave my mouth, I look at Edward and grin. He bursts out laughing and I quickly follow. Shaking his head, he jumps up and grins. "Good for them, that's what I say. Anyway, haven't we got some R&R to indulge in?"

Nodding, I head back to my room and not for the first time feel envious of my mother. She certainly knows how to have a good time. Maybe I should follow in her footsteps rather than worrying about where they are heading. At least she's living life to the full.

Now my main worry is how to look presentable in a bikini. Maybe the resort gym could use a new visitor. I'll check it out later and take the first step towards taking back control of my body.

By the time I emerge from my room looking semi-presentable, Edward is already by the pool. I feel like a lottery winner must feel as I regard the hunk of a man splayed out on his sunbed. Wow, I can't tear my eyes away from that body. Once again, my imagination goes into a feeding frenzy as I imagine all sorts of deprivation with this amazing specimen.

Luckily for me, the dark shades I'm wearing disguises where I am firmly looking and I try to appear unaffected as I lay my towel out on the bed next to him.

"Hey, Edward. Do you want me to do your back?"

Immediately the words leave my mouth I wish they hadn't. Why did I offer to place my hands on him in a massaging manner? I'm so desperate it's embarrassing.

Edward seemingly thinks nothing of it because he smiles and throws me the factor 30. "Thanks, if you don't mind."

He sits up with his back to me and I take a deep breath. Me and my big mouth. Mind you, this could be the most fun I've had in years and will stoke my night time fantasies for the next ten years.

I set about my mission pretending it's Ryan or Saskia. *Nothing to see here. Just one friend doing another a favour. Go about your business and carry on.*

The trouble is, my head is shouting but my heart can't hear it. I am enjoying the feeling of Edwards hard body beneath my fingers way too much and rub away with pure pleasure. It's been so long since I've had a man under these fingers and I am relishing every groan-inducing minute of it.

Edwards' skin feels hard and toned and his muscles hard and taut. His head rolls to the side as I reach his neck and he says deeply, "Wow, Amanda, have you trained as a masseur at all in life. If not, I think you've found your calling."

His words bring me back to reality and I say with embarrassment. "Sorry, years of scrubbing the work surfaces and leathering off the windows. I suppose household chores count as training for something."

He laughs and turning around says impishly, "My turn now."

What?! Oh my God, fantasy alert. Will my body remember not to betray me in a public place?

Shrugging, I throw him the cream. "Knock yourself out."

I turn around and think I hold my breath as I wait for the pressure of a man's much-desired touch on my bare skin.

Then the miracle happens and Edwards hands are touching me and pressing into me with precision and care. He obviously takes his smearing duties seriously because he is way more thorough than me. Can life really get any better? I am so living the dream this week.

Then it's over and he says with satisfaction.

"There you go. I can't have my best travel companion burnt to a crisp, can I?"

Smiling, I settle back on my sunbed and fully intend on re-living the moment for the rest of the day.

CHAPTER 28

About two hours later I hear a familiar voice shouting at me from the water. "Hey, Amanda. What are you doing lazing around? We need your ball skills."

I open my eyes and hear Edward laughing softly beside me as Chase shouts from the water.

Grinning, I sit up and shake my head.

"Hi, guys. You must be seriously bored to want to play with me again."

Nate shouts. "What ya talkin' about. You're awesome and can sure handle a ball."

Edward laughs a little louder and flashes me an amused look. I fix him with a challenging stare and say, "You up for it?"

His eyes sparkle and he laughs softly. "I'm sort of looking forward to witnessing your ball skills for myself first-hand."

He winks which makes me feel all flustered and maidenly. Chase shouts, "Yeah, Amanda you can play on my team and your brother can play with Nate."

Edward rolls his eyes as I giggle. This should be fun.

And it is. For the next thirty minutes, we indulge in a youthful game of water polo. The guys are such good fun and I love spending time with them. Life for them is one endless party and they appear never down or sullen like my own children. Once again, I wonder if this is the norm in Florida. Life here appears easy and carefree without the usual tests that life throws at us.

Edward turns out to be quite the athlete and I enjoy watching him. I'm not sure why I appear to have taken to this game so much because like Chase says, I'm a natural. I score many a winning punch and we win quite easily.

At the end Chase and Nate invite us for a drink at the lakeside pool which we accept gratefully.

We sit around on some barstools at the swim up pool bar and Chase looks at us with interest. "Are all English people such good sports?"

I shrug. "Who knows? I bet given half the chance they would at least try."

Nate looks at Edward. "Hey, man, you tried the gym here yet?"

Edward shakes his head. "Not yet, I may head over later and give it a try."

Chase looks at me. "How about you Amanda? Do you fancy it?"

Mentally shaking away the thought of what I can't stop fancying I nod. "Sounds cool."

Edward raises his eyes and I giggle inside. Living among teenagers rubs off sometimes and I often find myself adopting their youthful language. All it does is make me look like someone trying way too hard but it can't be helped.

I look over at Chase and say with interest, "So guys, what are your plans when you return home?"

Chase grins at Nate who says, "Off to Jefferson County College. We're both in the football team and got scholarships there. When we start, it'll be full on 24/7. It's the best college in the state for football and slackers don't last long there."

I'm impressed and say sadly, "I wish my son had a purpose. All he wants to do is play on his X box."

Chase looks interested. "How old is he?"

"18. He's at college doing computer science. I'm not sure he knows what he wants to do afterward but at least he's focusing on something he enjoys I suppose."

The guys nod. "Yeah, that helps. You got any other kids?"

"Yes, a daughter, Saskia. She's 16 and in her final year at school. I think she wants to go to college, but she hasn't decided what to do yet. Any suggestions I make are shot down in flames."

Chase nods. "Yeah, I have a brother like that. He's younger than me but doesn't want to do anything other than play on his computer. He'll come good though."

He turns to Edward. "How about you, man? You got any kids?"

He shakes his head. "No, I never had the chance."

The guys shrug and Nate says, "There's still time."

Edward laughs. "I doubt that but it's fine. I get an easy life because of it."

The guys turn to grab some more beers and I catch Edward's eye. He smiles but I see a tinge of sadness there that wasn't there before. Of course, he has missed out on a family of his own and a life that most of us take for granted. I never really thought about that side of his loss before.

We stay for another drink before promising the guys we'll check out Disney Springs later. They appear addicted to the place and I suppose it would be good to add that to the list of places to visit.

We head back for lunch and Edward says, "I may go to the gym later. I need to work on my fitness and it's as good as time as any."

I nod. "Yes, I may join you if that's ok? I did belong to one, but I was rubbish at attending. Maybe it's time to embrace the new me and turn over a new leaf."

Decision made, I vow to make this just one of my new regimes for the new me. It's time to whip this body back into pre-children shape and the only casualty that I care about is the fact I will have to forego my daily dose of Krispy Kreme's.

As soon as I get back to the apartment, I head to Skype to try to locate my mother. Once again, it just rings and my heart sinks. Where is she? Instead, I call Tina in the hope she's free and luckily, she answers on the second try.

As her familiar face fills the screen, I smile with relief. She grins, "Hi, babe. You're looking amazing. The Florida sun obviously agrees with you."

I roll my eyes. "As if? I must look like some sort of out-of-control monster mum. I've spent the morning in the pool playing water polo and must have wrinkles on wrinkles because of it."

She shakes her head. "No, I'm not joking. You really are looking amazing. You look rested and the tan you're getting is making you look healthy and happy."

She narrows her eyes. "Unless something else - or someone else is the reason. Go on, put me out of my misery and tell me you're *at it* with his hotness."

Quickly, I look around to see that he isn't loitering again and whisper, "I'm not going to lie, the thought does cross my mind several times a day but it's strictly business between us. He's like a no entry sign. One-way street, no two-way traffic allowed."

She looks surprised. "Why? Is he gay then?"

I shake my head and look at her sadly. "No, just lonely. He's coping with losing someone he loved and is in a fragile place. Just my luck really. Locked away with the hottest man I have ever met who is totally out of bounds." Tina looks sympathetic. "Never mind. Just enjoy your holiday while you can. You may not get another chance like this."

I nod. "I intend to. The trouble is, being here is heaven and hell. I want to enjoy this magical experience so much but the worries from home have followed me out here and are making me lose my mind."

She looks concerned. "Still not heard from your mother?"

Shaking my head, I say with a worried voice. "Last I heard she was setting sail with a crew of Jolly Rogers where it would appear all connections to civilisation are severed. She has gone against protocol and broken off into some sort of fringe group and may be expelled as a result. I bet she's the ringleader, it's her all over. However, that's not even the worse thing."

Tina looks interested. "Ooh, go on. I can't wait for this one."

"It's bad, Tina. I befriended my children on Instagram masquerading as an alter ego. I fashioned myself into someone they would be interested in and all I've done is make one of them interested in me in a very disturbing way."

She laughs. "Tell me everything."

"Well, Ryan has become obsessed with my alter ego and is currently stalking her."

Grabbing my phone, I scroll to Brandy's page and

hold it up to the screen. "See, this is the person he apparently thinks is his soulmate."

As I look at the page, I see a comment on my latest photo and with a sinking feeling see it's from Ryan. Turning to Tina, I groan. "Oh my god, he's messaging her now."

"Quickly read it and don't leave anything out."

As I start reading I can't believe what he's written.

"Hey Brandy. Love your posts we have so much in common. PM me your Snapchat and we can connect."

I look at Tina in horror and she laughs fit to burst. "Oh my god, Mandy Moo. Only you could make your own son fall in love with you without him knowing."

I groan. "What do I do now? He's made contact, I have to say something. I don't have a Snapchat and am not about to get one anytime soon either."

Tina looks at me thoughtfully. "I think you need to post a picture of a hot guy. I don't know, someone superhot and say he's your boyfriend. I bet he'll leave you alone then."

I think about it for a moment and then grin as the solution hits me. "I know just the guy. You're a genius, Tina."

She blows me a kiss. "Glad to be of assistance. Anyway, I had better go because Derek and I are booked in for a couple's massage. It does strange things to my libido so I expect we're be at it all afternoon."

Once again, I pretend to gag and she laughs. "You're just jealous because I can. Have fun searching for supercute guys to be your boyfriend – Brandy!"

She closes the screen leaving me with the solution to my Brandy problem. Now I just need to find Chase.

CHAPTER 29

After a light lunch, Edward and I head to the gym. I take my phone just in case I see a hot guy to pose as my boyfriend – sorry Brandy's boyfriend. Tina's right, this solution is pure genius.

I am pleased to see a running machine available as that's the only thing I can do. I am actually feeling really good about myself at the moment. I've had a nice rest today and Tina's right, my skin's looking tanned and healthy. I've pulled my hair back into a ponytail and brought my headphones. I even feel healthier out here and far from dreading this session, I'm actually looking forward to it.

So, as Edward hits the weights I start running like Forrest Gump. I plug in my headphones and set off at a brisk pace. As the tunes fill my ears, I totally tune out. In my mind I am super fit woman. The new me is fearless and brave. She runs like a pro and nothing brings her down. This new me is energetic and healthy. She eats muesli for breakfast and exists on a banana and a protein shake for lunch. Dinner is a salad followed by grilled chicken and a healthy fruit salad. Yes, this is the life. Brandy is my new best friend because I am morphing into her as we speak.

For most of my run I fantasise about life as Brandy. I catch tantalising glimpses of Edward in the mirror as he works up a sweat and imagine our life together. We are a super couple who live life as an adventure. We don't have kids, just experiences and every day is filled with new travels and lots of hot sex.

I run a little faster and enjoy my new life. This is what I want in my future. A life filled with realised dreams and challenges. A life walking beside the man I love and who loves me more than air. We will share our dreams and enjoy life to the full. This is what I want, and it's up to me to make it happen. The trouble is, in three days' time I will be back to Tescos and Edward will be heading off somewhere else with another middle-aged desperado with the same crisis as me.

For the first time in my life, I last a full hour in the gym. I suppose it's because I was so intent on living life as Brandy I was even loathe to give that up. As we walk back to the apartment Edwards says, "I was impressed, Amanda. You did well to keep going back there."

Shrugging, I try to hide the flush of pleasure his praise brings me. "Oh, you know, it was nothing. I spend so much time running around after my children that was easy."

He nods and as we reach the apartment, he grins and says lightly, "Anyway once we're ready we can hit the mall. I'm sure this is one activity you know a lot more than me about."

I shake my head sadly. "I wish, Edward. All my money is spent in the place where I earn it. The only shopping I ever get to do is in Tescos and I've got the bills to prove it. In fact, I can't even remember the last time I had a real shopping spree."

He looks thoughtful. "Oh well, maybe this is that time. What do you need, one hour?"

Nodding, I follow him inside. This afternoon is going to be torture for more than just the reason I want to launch myself at Edward at every given opportunity. No, this will be torture because even more than I love Krispy Kreme doughnuts, I love shopping and with limited funds, this will be excruciating.

Even the shops in Orlando are the proverbial dream come true. Designer brands at bargain prices and clearance rails in every shop. The sun beats down on us as we peruse the delights set inside the designer outlet grid.

It feels strange to be shopping in such heat and I decide this is how the perfect people must live. Foreign holidays with limitless credit cards to indulge their every whim and fancy. Just for a moment I pretend to be one of them. Brandy is definitely a perfect person and I wish I had thought of this years ago. When I feel down, I can pretend to be her. Nobody will ever know, except those I choose to share my alter egos life.

We head inside many shops and I stare with envy at the amazing creations on offer. I wish I had a budget to cope with this extravaganza but I don't.

Instead I help Edward choose some new boots and a thick leather belt. I am tempted to buy Saskia a new t-shirt and Ryan a hoodie though. I can say they were gifts from the Lake District. I'm sure they have shopping villages there too.

Edward takes many photographs and I look with envy at the masses of designer bags being paraded around by satisfied shoppers. If anything, this just reinforces my resolve to step my life up a gear and make it count. I want to live my life like this and it's up to me to make it happen. I'm sure my new salary as a manager will be a good starting point.

After a while, Edward looks at me thoughtfully.

"You know, it would be good to have a selection of bags for the photos. I don't know, a shot of you carrying them from behind or something. Some of the more coveted brands would be good."

I nod in agreement. "Yes, maybe we could ask the stores for a free bag in exchange for a mention in your article. It's free advertising for them so I can't see there being a problem."

He nods. "Ok you take one side and I'll take the other. We'll meet outside Timberland for a photo by the fountain."

He heads off and I look around me with a critical eye. Now, what would most people be interested in?

I head inside the first store of a well-known designer and explain to the sales assistant my purpose. As I thought she was only too happy to oblige and in no time at all I have amassed quite a collection. If only they had the actual shopping in them, I would be a happy bunny.

It's difficult to ignore the bargains clamouring for my attention along the way but the thought of the credit card bill at the end puts paid to any temptation.

I see Edward waiting by the fountain and once again my heart flutters. He looks super cool with his smart shorts and tight-fitting t-shirt. Once again, his designer stubble is calling to the wanton woman in me and the sight of those muscles straining against his shirt is sending my hormones into a frenzy. Thankfully, I have my large shades on and can blame the flush in my cheeks on the humidity.

He watches me approach and I lose my mind. I am now the most tortured woman in existence. Hot guy, hot place and hot shopping. The trouble is, none of it belongs to me so all I can do is dream.

He smiles and looks with appreciation at the bundle of bags in my arms.

"Good, looks like you've been successful. Now let's fluff them out as if there are things in them and load you up."

We set about our task and it doesn't take long before I'm ready and looking every inch the perfect shopper. I start walking away from the fountain with an added wiggle for Edwards' benefit. A girl can dream can't she and as I'm now a supermodel I must play the part. The fact it's my rear view is a godsend. I can at least pretend to be perfect all the time they can't see my face.

It doesn't take long and Edward smiles happily.

"Great, we're done here. Is there anywhere else you want to go while we're here?"

Wishing it was an option, I just smile. "No, I think I'm done."

We head back to the apartment armed with enough empty carriers to fill a recycling container on their own and feel very satisfied by a job well done.

CHAPTER 30

We decide to head to Disney Springs for the evening to see what all the fuss is about. Chase and Nate told us about a great bar that serves cocktails and has live music. I actually can't remember the last time I went out on the town with a man and take a great deal of time with my outfit. I feel refreshed and re-energised after the morning's rest and am looking forward to a night out with a hot man.

Edward almost makes me drool when I head into the communal part of the apartment. He's wearing a loose white short-sleeved shirt and smart dark grey shorts. His hair is tousled and his face is showing the stubble of a man that doesn't have to try very hard.

We have fallen into an easy friendship and it's a world apart from the angry beginning that feels like a lifetime ago. As I approach, I feel him looking me up and down and smile inside. Maybe he's not as immune to me as he likes to pretend. I've seen the odd look of interest followed by a quick glance away. I saw him checking me out in the gym as I ran which gave me the motivation to keep going. And I've seen the way his glance lingers as I enter a room and follows me when I leave it. Yes, Edward Bastion may not be looking for love but he's a man after all. I'm betting he's as desperate as I am for a bit of company now and again. How I wish I was brave enough to approach him but he's made it pretty clear he's not interested in that kind of woman. So, with an inward sigh, I smile at him brightly.

"All set?"

Nodding, he grabs his keys, and we set off for Disney Springs.

Once again, I fall in love with a place as soon as I set eyes on it. Disney Springs is a mini village consisting of shops to tempt the child in all of us and some to tempt the adults into parting with their hard-earned dollars. Various restaurants hug the edge of a large lake and it is styled as a Mediterranean palazzo with mosaics and fountains around which are village style buildings. The heat is still intense, and the sun beats a steady path to my core, warming me through and making me feel more relaxed than I have felt in years.

We decide to head to a little jetty where a bar sits some way out on a pier. We can sit surrounded by water and feel the cool breeze of the lake as we watch the world go by. Edward orders us some refreshing drinks and we sit in a comfortable silence as we 'people watch.' The sun sparkles on the water and I look at Edward with a smile. "You know, I love this place so much. Not just Disney Springs but everywhere we've been. You are so lucky this is your job."

Edward nods. "I suppose I am. I've sort of forgotten about that sometimes. It all blends into one and most of the time I just long for the week to be over so I can head home back to normality."

I decide to delve a little deeper into his life. "So, where's home exactly?"

He sips his drink and leans back. "London. I live in Chiswick because it's not far from my offices. It suits me because everything I need is on my doorstep."

"So, what do you do in your spare time?"

"The usual. I head home late, throw in a ready meal and then head to the gym or out for drinks with friends."

I stare at him with fascination. "Do you ever get lonely living on your own?"

He looks out over the water and a lost look casts a shadow over his face. I think I must hold my breath because I can see him battling with something he's not sure whether to say or not. Instead, he shrugs and fixes me with a wry grin. "Of course. I am a human being after all, despite what you may hear to the contrary. I know what it's like to share your life with someone who means the world to you. That's what makes it harder. Nobody I have ever met has ever measured up to Karen."

I feel my heart sink as he looks at me and smiles softly.

"Do you know, Amanda? You are the only woman I've ever told any of this to. I'm a very private person and don't like to let anyone in. For some reason though you're different to the others. I feel comfortable with you and just want to let you know I've enjoyed this week more than you'll ever know."

I smile and lean my head to one side saying cheekily. "Despite ignoring me, freezing me out and nearly having me killed, I've enjoyed your company too, Edward. Thanks for such a memorable trip and I'll miss this adventure when it's over."

Edward looks thoughtful and then leans forward and stares at me. "Who says it has to be over?"

I just stare at him in surprise as he says softly.

"I always need a travel companion to act as my model and holidaymaker. Why can't you be that person? We get along and could have so much fun travelling the world and writing about it. What do you say, Amanda, are you up for it?"

I just stare at him in total shock. Well, I never saw this one coming. He laughs. "It's not like you to be speechless. Is it such a dreadful prospect?"

Just for a moment, I fall into the trap he's set me. I envision a life globe-trotting with this handsome man beside me. We will grow close and then become inseparable. Friendship will turn to love and nothing will ever divide us. Then reality crashes me back down to earth and the tears threaten to blind me. Edward looks at me with concern and says with a worried voice, "I haven't said anything wrong, have I?"

I shake my head and smile through my tears. "No, it's a wonderful idea. I would love nothing more and if it was just me, I would leap at the opportunity. The trouble is, it isn't just me. I come with a package and they still need me. I have to put my children first and provide stability in their life where it was destroyed. They are at a vulnerable age and I need to be there for them. Thank you so much for the opportunity but this is one dream I'll have to wake up from. Women like me have to be realistic and accept their path in life. Maybe when they are settled, I can start again, live my life like I want to. But they aren't settled and I'm not free to do what I want, even though my ex-husband appears to have done just that. You need someone with no baggage and the freedom to follow you around with no restrictions."

We just stare at each other and I feel my heart sink. Way to go Amanda. Look a gift horse in the mouth and punch it hard. So much for new beginnings. Whether I like it or not, I'm a mother first and foremost and the girl I was will have to accept the woman I am now.

Edward looks worried and I smile brightly. "So, we must make the most of this week while we're still here. Let's just make it count and give us some memories to see me through the management training programme in my future."

Edward smiles but I sense the disappointment in him. He looked so excited when he asked me and just for a moment, I believed it could happen. Then my responsibilities claimed me once again, and the dream faded as quickly as it began. Oh well. Never mind. Maybe in a few more years, you never know.

CHAPTER 31

Ok, I'm now out of control and should be arrested by the respectability police. Something triggered inside me when Edward asked me to travel with him. It was the realisation that I only have a few more days to be the girl I was, before the woman I am comes back to claim me.

I think I dragged poor Edward to every bar/cum nightclub in the whole of Disney Springs. We met up with Chase and Nate at the karaoke bar and I took many pictures for Brandy's album and posed with the guys in shots that a woman of my age had no business taking.

Edward appears to be enjoying himself but now and then I see a worried shadow pass across his face as he looks at me.

It must be 10pm by the time Chase pulls me on the dance floor and we let rip. I managed to join the free Wi-Fi and post several shots of him looking super fit and every inch the successful football star that he aspires to be. This should deter Ryan from thinking he has a chance with Brandy. I'm a genius.

The drinks keep on coming and soon even Edward relaxes and joins in the fun. We decide to call a cab to take us back to the hotel and set about drinking the night away and behaving like the irresponsive teenagers we are partying with. The fact that we look like their mum and dad is irrelevant. They don't care and neither should I. It's all in the name of friendship and Instagram, anyway.

I am quite proud that I manage to get through the whole of *'Spice up your life'* without forgetting the words. The fact they are before me on the screen doesn't even come into it. I like to freestyle and move around the stage like Ginger Spice. Edward and the boys laugh and cheer me on and take lots of photos to embarrass me with later.

Edward keeps the cocktails coming and coupled with the heat and the company I think this is actually the best night of my life.

We move on to the club next door and I don't even feel like I stick out. All ages and nationalities are here and multicultural Britain has nothing on the League of Nations within these four walls. We mingle with Germans, Canadians and even a couple of Russians tempt us with some vodka shots. The fact that Chase and Nate are so amenable and easy going helps enormously. They don't seem to care who they speak to and my British reserve has been left firmly at the door.

I even manage a bit of flamenco dancing on a table cheered on by Edward and the guys. I can't believe how free I feel. It's as if Amanda Swallows, mother and general dogsbody doormat, ceases to exist. I am party animal woman about town who takes life by the horns and shakes it in a flamenco dance.

Edward also appears to be having a great time. His

usual reserve was left with my morality at the door and he parties on down with the rest of us. The guys challenge him to a shots competition and they do that man thing where they all huddle together cheering as each one takes a shot. America really is the land of the free. You can do anything here in the name of vacation and are welcomed with open arms. I can just see Alf, the landlord of the Spotted Dog, allowing this sort of behaviour. He would have called for the local police to storm the premises by now and arrest us for a public order offence.

As the night draws to a close, the clubs tone it down, and we are left swaying on the dance floor to the Power of Love. Somehow Edward and I have managed to cling to each other as we sway around the near-empty dance floor, holding each other up as we go. I giggle and whisper, "You know, Edward. If we were one of those super celebrity couples like Brangelina, we would be known as Edam."

Edward grins. "A bit cheesy, don't you think?"

I laugh and snuggle in further. I'm not going to lie; I am enjoying myself way too much and lean into him shamelessly. He doesn't appear to care though and his hand holds me close rubbing circles on my lower back.

I burrow into him even further and allow my head to rest on his manly chest. His arms wrap around me in a protective shield and I think I must be dreaming because, at this moment in time, everything in my life is perfect. It's only when I see a confused look shared between Nate and Chase that I realise we are not behaving like a pair of siblings. I burst out laughing as Edward looks at me with surprise. Nodding over to the boys, I whisper, "I think they're a little disturbed by our floor show. You are supposed to be my brother after all."

Edward grins wickedly and whispers. "Then we should give them something to really talk about."

I look at him in surprise as he leans his face towards mine. Then dreams do come true in the land of wishes because in a Nanosecond Edward's lips are on mine and I shamelessly let him. He pulls me even closer as we kiss in full view of the hardened partygoers. Wow! Kissing Edward is like being in a film or something. I swear fireworks explode around me as I kiss him back with everything I've got. Somehow, we stop dancing and just kiss each other with a passion that has been contained for far too many years. Now I can't stop. The music stops but we don't. The lights come on but we carry on. It's only when we hear a nervous, "Hey, guys. Um... I'm not sure you realise this, Ed but you're actually kissing your sister."

We pull apart and grin as we note the shock on the boy's faces. Then Nate shakes his head and says in awe, "Wow, Europeans are far out."

Giggling, I hold Edward's hand and come clean. "It's ok guys, we're not really brother and sister. I just made that up to explain why I hated him."

Chase looks confused and now completely sober. Mind you, I think the shock of what's just happened has sobered us all up. Edward laughs and thankfully just holds my hand a little tighter. "We're business colleagues on a work trip. I was a complete ass to Amanda when we arrived and she hated me on sight. Luckily for me, I have won her over and proved that I'm not such a monster after all. The trouble is, she won't give me a second chance and is leaving me in two days' time."

Chase shakes his head and laughs. "Whoa, I knew you guys were awesome, but this is something else."

He turns to me and grins. "Well, you can't say no to

him now. You've sealed the deal in front of witnesses."

As I look at the three of them looking at me with so much hope I feel my world spiralling out of control. On one hand, I want Edward more than life itself. He's everything I've ever wanted and more. The trouble is, we are drunk in a foreign land which counts for zero back at home. There I have responsibilities and people depending on me. Edward travels all the time and I have no business thinking I could be part of it, no matter how much I want to. So, I just smile sadly and squeeze his hand and say what most cowards do. "We'll see."

The guys cheer but I see the sadness in Edward's eyes. He knows it's an impossible dream. Out here it's a sure thing and may even work for a few months when we return. The trouble is, real life has a habit of winning and the mundane takes over. The best thing for all concerned will be to part as friends and take with us our happy memories of the week when I was free to live again.

We manage to stagger back, via the back of a cab and the two people who left the apartment were very different to the two who return. It must be 3am but sleep is of no consequence. I feel nervous as I sense that everything has just changed between us.

As Edward lets us in, we both stand awkwardly in the little lobby of the apartment and just stare at each other. He looks a little worried and I smile shyly. "You know, I really enjoyed myself tonight. I hope I didn't come on too strong. It's not that I get many opportunities like that, so I think I crammed them all into one night. I'm sorry if I've made things awkward between us. You must be cursing your luck being stuck with yet another middle-aged desperate housewife."

Edward just looks at me and his eyes twinkle in the dusky light. He takes my hand and kisses it gently and then says softly. "I regret nothing, Amanda. I've wanted to do that for several days now. You surprise me every day with what a very special person you are. I think everything changed when you went water skiing. I've never seen anyone so brave and full of courage in my life. The fact you were so proud and did it to put me in my place impressed me no end. I find you funny, interesting and the kindest person I have ever met. You put others before yourself and you don't even realise just how beautiful you really are."

I hear his words but I think he must be saying them to someone behind me. Either that or he's drunk way more than I first thought. He steps a little closer and pulls me towards him. He tilts my face to his and whispers, "Let's start again here and now. We still have two days for me to convince you this is the life for you. Will you let me at least try?"

I look at him shyly and nod. "I would like that."

Then he lowers his lips to mine and kisses me so softly and sweetly my legs almost give way. Then he pulls back and says huskily, "Good night, Amanda. Thanks for the best evening I've had in a very long time."

I just smile and turn towards my room in disbelief. Edward just called me beautiful. I actually can't remember when I was last called that. Certainly not in a very long time. I've forgotten how much it means to be referred to in that way. When Edward looked at me it wasn't at a middle-aged housewife and mother. He looked at me like a man looks at a woman. In that moment I felt desired and as he said - *beautiful*. Just those few words have changed everything.

CHAPTER 32

I am having an amazing dream about travelling the world with Edward who looks like Brad Pitt when that weird skypy sound interrupts it. Groaning, I reach out and grab the offending device.

I shuffle into a sitting position and open it, blinking as the light of the screen hits my tortured eyes. Then I see Saskia looking at me with total horror as she gasps, "Oh my god, mum. What's happened to you? You look terrible."

Quickly, I try to fluff out my hair and say briskly. "Sorry, I must have fallen asleep for a bit. Um… these hill walks take a lot out of me."

She rolls her eyes. "Well, I must say it's not much of an advert for walking holidays. You look wrecked and your face has gone all leathery. Why on earth didn't you book yourself into a spa or something?"

She rolls her eyes. "Anyway, I just wanted to tell you that Nicola and I are finished."

I look at her in surprise and am pleased to note that she appears unaffected by the situation.

I say gently. "What happened?"

She sniffs. "He turned out to be everything I hate in a man. He was ok all the time we were kissing but when that excitement faded, I realised just how boring he was. I mean, when you compare him to Brandy's boyfriend there's zero competition."

I say weakly, "Brandy?"

She looks excited. "You remember I told you about that Instagram blogger Ryan and me are following. Well, it turns out she's living my dream life. Not only is she in Orlando at Disney but her boyfriend is the hottest guy I have ever seen. You should see the pics of their night out. Well, it made me realise that life is for living and there must be no settling for substandard companions. I fully intend on applying for the Disney college programme as soon as I get away from this hell hole and make my life count for something."

My head is buzzing with this new information and I say weakly, "What about Ryan? I thought he was stalking her."

She shakes her head. "When he saw the total hottie she's dating, he went into one of his sulks. He's been glued to her feed all day hoping it was just some random guy and not what we all know. I'm a little worried though because he's been asking dad about battle re-enactment life. I think he wants to picture Brandy's boyfriend as the enemy and pulverise him on the battlefield. Typical boy thinks fighting solves everything."

Blinking, I try to focus on my daughter's words and not listen to the banging in my head that seems to be gaining in intensity. Saskia peers even closer. "You know, mum, you do look terrible. Are you sure you're not ill or something? I mean, you're always in bed these days."

I see her worried face and try to reassure her. "No, it's like I said, I'm just worn out with all the hiking."

Shaking her head, she looks past me and frowns. "Ok, I told you I was calling mum. Can't you even let me have five minutes without bothering me."

She pulls a face. "You know, I never realised how annoying dad can be. He's trying to make me do all sorts over here. When have I ever had to do the washing up? I mean, it's child slave labour. And so what if I need the time to paint my nails instead of helping make the beds or prepare the food? I'm telling you, mum, this isn't normal life out here. Dad's turned into some sort of Victorian style father. Doesn't he know things are different now?"

I say softly. "The trouble is, Saskia, he's right. I've never pushed either of you to step up and take control of things. You're too used to me fetching and carrying for you and allowing you both to escape the realities of life. Maybe this week will do you both good and make you see just what life's about."

Saskia looks worried. "Mum stop, you're scaring me. Something is badly wrong with you. Not only do you look absolutely terrible but now you're talking nonsense. Maybe you should call a doctor or something, you're obviously delirious."

She smiles as if she's some sort of caring angel daughter and blows me a kiss. "Anyway, I must go because we're going out for lunch. You know, mum, Sunday can't come soon enough for me."

Then she looks at me with the face of the little girl she was and says softly, "I do miss you, mum. Life isn't the same without you. It feels empty and strange and it's weird you're not with us. I can't relax with dad and Lucy like I can with you."

Her face falls as she says sadly, "I love you, mum. See you soon."

Then she is gone, leaving me in a complete and utter state of shock. Did she just say she loved and missed me? And that face. The little girl that looked at me I thought was lost forever. It was that same look she used to give me when I read to her at night and she smiled sweetly as I kissed her goodnight. The same look when she ran out of school and into my arms and the same look when she was ill and I held her close to me in my bed. She is in there still battling between childhood and adulthood.

Her call has made me even more homesick and now everything seems wrong. What am I doing? My children need me at home where I can love and protect them. What was I thinking running off with a stranger and daring to think I could have a life of my own? That life ceased to exist when I became a mother. Surely that's the law, isn't it? Put your children first and to hell with the consequences?

Then my heart speaks up and whispers, "Ignore what your head is saying. You deserve this little bit of happiness. Don't let it go because when those children leave, you will be on your own. You owe it to yourself to be happy. Don't listen to your head, your heart knows best."

I flop back onto the pillows and squeeze my eyes tightly shut. What on earth am I supposed to do?

CHAPTER 33

When I finally venture out of my room, looking a little more human than when I first woke up, the apartment is empty. I'm so used to seeing Edward tapping on his iPad that it throws me a little. I wonder if he's still asleep. Maybe I should go and check but that would be invading his personal space - wouldn't it?

Instead, I set about making a coffee and hope that if I clatter around loudly enough, he will venture forth from his man cave.

By the time the coffee's made he still hasn't surfaced, so I take it out on the balcony and sit looking out over the view of the lake. As I sit there many thoughts race through my head. *Edward kissed me and seemed to enjoy it!* He asked me to travel with him. *Saskia has ditched Nicola because of Chase.* Ryan is heartbroken and set on a killing revenge spree. *I want to take Edward up on his offer.* I'm a mother put yourself last. *I'm a woman and I have needs.* I don't want to join the management training programme. *Where is my mother?* I want Brandy's life....

I sit contemplating everything as my coffee grows cold. Nothing makes sense and I know I'm at a crossroads in life. Can I really put myself first and take Edward up on his offer? I want to. It would be the first time in my life I did.

I am interrupted by the sound of the door opening and look up to see Edward coming in balancing two take-out coffees on a box of Krispy Kreme's. He smiles when he sees me waiting and places them on the table. "I thought you may need a strong coffee after last night and some sugar for your energy levels."

I smile happily and almost fall onto the doughnuts in my haste to shove one in my mouth. I knew he was the man for me. He's good I'll give him that. One Krispy Kreme and I'm anybodys.

After polishing one off almost whole, I groan. "You certainly know what makes me tick, Edward. But then again, I suppose I have dropped enough hints."

He laughs. "Just a few. Anyway, how are you feeling this morning? Ready for another full-on day as a tourist?"

I look at him with excitement. "Yes, I am. I know it was a late one but I'm conscious we only have a few more days to pack it all in. I don't want to miss a minute of it."

I see his eyes narrow and he looks a little sad. "I wish you would reconsider my offer, Amanda. I'm sure we could work things around your children and the pay is good, not to mention the perks."

I take a sip of my coffee and think about what he's said. Maybe I should try. I want to. But then again, we have only known each other for a few days. I have the chance to join a management programme and make something of my life. Ordinary people like me don't get to live the dream. He would soon find out that I'm one of them and not perfect like he deserves.

I look at him thoughtfully. "I would like to. Let's just see how this week goes and when the dust settles on our return, we could meet up and see if it's still an option. I mean, by the end of this week you will probably hate me as much as you did at the beginning of it."

To my surprise, Edward leans across the table and takes my hand. It feels nice and I look at him in surprise and smile shyly. He looks into my eyes and I can't tear my gaze away as he says huskily, "I meant every word I said last night and will spend the rest of this trip proving it could work. You could say the tables have turned and now it's me pursuing my travel companion and not the other way around. I won't rest until you have seen how good it could be between us."

I think we just stare at each other for what seems like an eternity before I smile and break the spell. "So, what delights do you have planned for today?"

He pulls back and grins. "Kennedy Space Center. To be honest this is a bit of a selfish one. I've always wanted to go there so used this as an excuse. I think you'll enjoy it."

I smile and eye up another Krispy Kreme, wondering if it would be greedy to have two. He pushes it toward me and winks. "Here you go, you may as well finish this one while I grab my iPad and see if we've heard from the moneypennies."

I watch with interest as I devour the sugar-coated nectar of the gods. He studies his emails for a second before looking at me with concern. Alarm bells ring loudly in my ears and I know that look. Something's happened.

The doughnut turns to dust in my mouth and I say shakily, "What is it?"

He pushes the iPad towards me and says kindly, "I'm sure everything is fine."

The words swim before my eyes as I try to make sense of them.

Dear Madam

I thought you may like to know that the fringe breakout group have returned to the fold hours before the flight leaves for home. All is well and they report having a lovely time.

Regarding Dorothy Swallows, however, she has decided to remain as the guest of Cyril Atkins on board the Jolly Roger for one more week. She has assured the group that she is in good hands and will document her journey to share with the other members on her return.

I hope this puts your mind at rest.

Anonymous

I look over at Edward's concerned face and shake my head. "Well, I can't say I'm surprised, really. She's always been a little adventurous and you know what Edward?"

He shakes his head. "What?"

I stand up and push my chair back from the table.

"What's good enough for my mother is good enough for me. I'm done with playing the perfect mother. Look where it's got me? A nervous bundle of guilt and self-doubt and a couple of kids who appear to pity me. Nobody has ever put me first and just carry on doing what they want - when they want. First Robert, then my kids and now my mother. Nobody thinks about my feelings and just go about their lives as they see fit and to hell with what others think. Well, that's me now. For the next few days at least, I can pretend to be free. Free from responsibility and free from the mundane. I don't ask for much and expect nothing in return. So, my dear angry friend. Show me what you're made of because I am ready."

Edward grins and says, "Then there isn't a minute to lose. Follow me, Amanda, because I am putting you first for once in your life and failure is not an option."

We grab our stuff and head out. First stop Kennedy Space Center.

CHAPTER 34

True to his word Edward pulls out all the stops. He is attentive and charming and nothing is too much trouble for him. We take many photos for the article and Brandy's Instagram account and I push any guilt I brought with me away and set about making the most of this amazing opportunity with this amazing man.

If I wasn't feeling it already my feelings for Edward deepen by the minute. So, this is what it's like? Finally, I have a man beside me who sets my pulse racing and my heart beating a little faster with just one penetrating look or light touch. I find myself craving his attention like a drug and find myself inching closer to him as the day goes on. It's as if my body is feeling the gravitational pull of his and I can't blame the fact we're at Kennedy for that. He is good company and we laugh often and find we have a similar sense of humour and share the same outlook on life.

By the end of the day, I am closer to Edward Bastion than I have been to a man in years – probably ever. I always heard that love can hit you like a thunderbolt and never really understood how. Now I know because by the time we make it back to the hotel, I am head over heels in love with the man beside me.

As I get ready for the evening, I feel safe and secure in the knowledge that nobody will call. Because of the time difference, this is the time they are all sleeping and I can relax knowing I won't have to face the pressures of home.

Instead, I take a moment to study Ryan's Instagram and once again worry about my baby boy. He is so much quieter than Saskia and keeps himself to himself. He doesn't chat like she does and I wonder sometimes what he talks to his friend Mungo about. I was pleased that he would be spending this week with his father. Maybe he can penetrate that confusing exterior and draw him out of himself. The trouble is, Robert's on his honeymoon and probably doesn't have the time.

Ryan's familiar face stares out at me from Cyber Space and I feel the guilt return with a vengeance. I need to step it up with him on my return. Find out what's going on inside that mind of his and try to steer him on a better path. Maybe we should look into career options and attend seminars together. He's of an age where he could go one of two ways. I need to give him focus and purpose and set him off on the path to fulfilment - not the mundane.

His photos show me little of the last week. He doesn't appear to have done anything he wants to shout about and so I scroll over to Saskia's for more information. Among the usual pouting selfies are a few wedding shots. There's one of the four of them and I look closer with interest. Robert and Lucy look happy and grudgingly I have to admit she looks beautiful. Her black hair has been styled in a sort of updo and her usual heavy makeup has been toned down and brings out the prettiness in her face. She is laughing at something Robert is saying and I feel a pang as I see what I've been missing out on all these years. He looks relaxed and happy and is staring at her with the eyes of a man totally besotted and in love. Did he ever look at me like that? I can't remember. I suppose he must have done but all I can see when I think of him is the frown and the irritation in his gaze. He always looked weary and as if he had the weight of the world on his shoulders.

Any loving looks we shared quickly disappeared when the children came along. I never had time to lavish him with affection because I used up all my supply on them. He was firmly at the bottom of the list when it came to time management and by the time the children were in bed I had almost passed out with exhaustion. He used to moan that I never had time for him and if we ever had sex it was out of duty on my part just to keep him quiet.

Why can I see everything so clearly now as I look at this photograph? What could I have done differently to change what happened? Should I have worked harder on our relationship and we would have a future together of shared dreams and happiness? Or should we never have married in the first place? Maybe he was never my soul mate like Karen was Edward's. Perhaps I ruined my life by taking the first offer that came my way and caused this broken family because of my bad choices. But then I wouldn't have my beautiful children who despite their teenage behaviour I love with everything I've got. Whatever decision I made was worth it because I have them.

A knock on the door interrupts my thoughts and as I

shout, "Come in," Edward pokes his head around it and I smile at him as he comes and sits beside me on the bed.

"Are you ok, Amanda? Are you still up for going out tonight or would you rather stay in and grab a takeout from the pizza place?"

I shake my head and smile softly. "No, let's go out. I'm actually feeling really hungry now and could murder a steak or something."

Edward laughs. "I don't think you'll have to go that far but I agree, space travel certainly works up an appetite."

He sees my phone in my hand and says with interest. "Is that your family?"

I look down at the photograph and pass the phone to him. "Yes, it's a photo of Robert and Lucy with the kids. They look happy, don't they?"

He nods and then says softly. "It must hurt to see it."

I look at him and shake my head. "Not really. I'm just happy for them. They look happy and in love and I was just trying to remember back to a time that he looked at me like that. The trouble is, the memory has faded and I can't remember that he ever did. It's a bit sad when you think about it. I should have stacks of memories like this one but I don't."

Edward puts his arm around me and squeezes my shoulder. He says softly, "I don't believe that for a second. I'm guessing that your husband loved you very much. The trouble is, life sometimes gets in the way and couples grow apart. We change as humans and it's such a gradual process we don't realise it's happening until we wake up one day and see things differently. I expect that happened with you. I don't have any children of my own but I imagine it's a full-time job. Sometimes, when we reach a milestone in life, we look back and wonder how we got there at all. At least you have your family. Your children will always love you and will be a part of your life forever, as will their father."

I smile and look back at the photograph. I don't know how it's happened but life with Robert seems like a world away in my past. He looks like a familiar stranger. Somebody I once knew and loved but moved away from many years ago. The children look kind of happy I guess. Well, as happy as any sulky teenager forced to play happy families with a stranger marrying their father. This must have been hard on them and I can't imagine what went through their minds this week.

Sighing, I turn the picture off and look at Edward and smile.

"I think we should head out. All of that space travel has made me hungry and the food out here is seriously making me forget that I was meant to be on a diet."

Edward smiles softly and something about the way he looks at me takes my breath away. He is looking at me like a man desires a woman. I mean, really desires her. He is looking at me like I imagined myself looking at Veg man as I watched him wielding his carrots. But this is something else. This man sitting beside me is real, not a figment of my imagination. Somehow the impossible has happened and somebody is actually looking at me as if I count. I hold my breath and countdown in my mind because I know something is going to happen with this man.

My heart starts beating faster as he pulls me closer and tilts my face to his. He pushes my hair back that has fallen across my face and lowers his lips to mine. This time he kisses me gently and with so much care I swear my toes curl up. Something alien to me is taking over my rationality and I lean into him and kiss him back with equal passion, if not more. He pulls me closer and I actually let him. I cling to him like a lifeline because that what he feels like. He feels safe and secure and as if I have reached land after a tempestuous storm. Edward Bastion is my future, I know that now because my heart has knocked out my head in one winning knockout punch. I don't know how it will happen but my life is about to change forever.

CHAPTER 35

When we actually manage to stop kissing Edward looks at me and smiles. "Do you still want to go out or shall we spend the evening here instead?"

My heart starts beating so rapidly I'm worried for it. Oh, my God. This could happen, here tonight. Finally, my dreams will turn to reality, it's all there in the look he's shooting me. Now I'm faced with what I wanted so desperately I'm not sure I'm ready. I think a thousand thoughts shoot around my head at once as I try to make sense of the situation I'm now in. Edward's meaning is clear. He wants me as a man wants a woman and suddenly every self-doubt and insecurity I have is shouting at me. I'm not ready for this... *I am so ready for this*. He can't see you naked... *he will see you naked*. You're rubbish in bed... *you've got this*.

He must sense my unease because his face softens and he smiles gently.

"Let's head out and eat and then maybe later we can continue where we've left off. That is, if you want to."

I see the sudden doubt in his eyes and I think my heart starts kickboxing me inside. It's screaming at me to dive in head first and take advantage of probably the only offer I'm ever going to get this side of the care home.

Reaching out I grasp his hand and smile. "Edward, the only doubt in my mind is whether I'm really what you want. I'm not an experienced woman of the world. Until a few days ago I was content with watching a boxed set of Fifty Shades for my kicks. The only man I've ever been with in that sense was my husband."

He looks shocked and I nod sorrowfully. "It's true. So, you see this is a big deal for me and yet I know I want to more than anything. So, maybe we should head out first and cool things down a little."

He smiles and says softly. "You think this is normal for me. Well, it's not. I'm not saying I haven't dated women and yes, that did involve more than kissing. But there's something special about you, Amanda, which is why I'm moving so fast on this. I only have a few days to convince you to give me a shot and make this work. However, I want you to be 100% sure of this before we do. I'm not about to rush something that I've been searching for so long."

He nods towards the door. "Listen. I'll just grab my things and meet you downstairs. I'll get the car cooled down and you can meet me down there when you're ready."

He leans down and kisses me a lingering sexy kiss that almost makes me change my mind and pull him forcibly down. Then he smiles and heads back out of the door leaving me a hot sexy mess.

Immediately, I hear the door click shut I'm on my

iPad like a wasp on jam. I need advice and fast and who better than my partner in crime, Tina.

Frantically I wait for the skypy noise to connect and hope she hasn't gone out for dinner yet – or worse, indulging in the very recreational activity that's on my mind.

With considerable relief on my part, her face soon fills the little screen next to mine and she looks at me and grins.

"Hey, Amanda. You're looking tanned and beautiful."

I shake my head. "No time for that, Tina. I've got an emergency to discuss."

Immediately, she looks concerned. "Oh no, it's not your mother is it, or the children?"

I groan. "Much worse."

Her eyes widen and I say slightly hysterically, "Edward wants to have sex with me."

Just for a moment, she looks a little shell-shocked and not sure if she heard correctly. Then a broad grin breaks out across her face and she almost screams, "Way to go, Amanda. You lucky thing. What are you waiting for then?"

I whisper hysterically, "Ssh, he'll hear you."

She peers closer to the screen. "Is he there then, waiting in your bed for your decision?"

I laugh and roll my eyes. "Of course not. He's waiting in the car. We're heading out to eat first, but what should I do?"

Now Tina rolls her eyes. "Go get it girl. I can't believe you're even asking me. This is the best thing that's happened to you in years. A hot guy, a hot country and a hot night of hot sex all guaranteed to make you hot under the collar. What's to worry about?"

I whisper, "But I haven't had sex in ages and never with anyone but Robert. What if I get it wrong? What if he's turned off when we actually begin? I mean, I'm hardly in the first flush of youth. This body has been inflated to bursting point – twice and then like a balloon let off around the room and left shrivelled and empty. Pregnancy does that to a woman and I've got the scars to prove it."

Tina giggles. "It will soon regain its shape when it's filled to capacity. I wouldn't worry about a little thing like that. I'm pretty sure you'll be too otherwise occupied to worry about your body."

I groan. "What if he wants to do it with the lights on? I never let Robert see me unless the blackout curtains were closed. What do people do these days, anyway? I'm so confused because I think things may have moved on since my day. Everything else has so why not that as well?"

Tina starts to laugh until the tears roll down her face and I stare at her crossly. "What? I'm just saying. Tina I'm no supermodel you know and am so out of shape I'm like the used-up Playdough nobody wants to play with anymore. What am I to do?"

Tina frowns and looks quite intimidating for once.

"Now listen to me, Amanda Swallows. You are going to forget everything you've just told me and concentrate on the moment. Let things happen naturally and don't over-think it. Edward must really like you and I can see why. You are just a little out of practice but it's like riding a bike. You won't even think about it and get swept away in the moment. Trust him and trust yourself. You owe this to yourself. It's about time you re-joined the human race and had some fun for once. Just go with your urges and the rest will happen naturally. Oh, and make sure I get a full report tomorrow, you lucky thing."

I smile weakly. "Yes, you're right, of course. I'm being silly, aren't I? I'm not old and have just reached my prime. It's time to face my fears and embrace my new life."

She gives me the thumbs up and says excitedly. "Now sort yourself out and go and do what nature intended. Don't over-think it and just enjoy the whole experience. Good luck hun. I'll be thinking of you."

She pulls a face. "Ugh, no I won't. That came out wrong. I'll now be very much trying not to think about you and sex on legs Edward hot pants sexy man. God, you're so lucky."

Smiling, I wave goodbye and take a deep breath. She's right. This is the moment I've been waiting for since the HRT kicked in. Why waste an opportunity like this over fear of my own inadequacies?

With a deep breath, I grab my bag and head out to join the man himself.

CHAPTER 36

We head out to a nice restaurant by the water's edge. Fairy lights are strung up all around and soft music is playing nearby. Edward orders me a cocktail and himself a beer and looks at me as if I'm the only woman in the world. I feel so amazing with him. He makes me feel sexy and desirable and even laughs at my jokes. Surely, it's not an act? For all I know this could be the usual run of events when he's on a trip. It may all have been a big story to have hot sex with his travel companions and he does this all the time. Maybe that's why the moneypennies are running out of options. He could be a serial shagger and I'm his next victim.

So many thoughts race through my mind and yet only one that counts. Who cares anyway? Like Tina pointed out, he's hot and sexy and I've thought of little else since I grew to like him after our shaky start. So what if I never see him again. I'll have the memory at least.

So, after a few more cocktails I finally relax and just enjoy his company. We do get on rather well and appear to like the same things. I find myself totally at ease with him and can't imagine life without him in it now.

Once again, I take a shot of the restaurant and post it on Instagram with the caption *'Hot nights in paradise #exciting #romantictimes #hungry'*

Edward laughs and winks as he reads it and I grin shamelessly. "Not quite what a mother wants her children reading but Brandy is an IT girl about town. Not a middle-aged housewife hurtling through a mid-life crisis in a foreign land."

Edward shakes his head. "We may have reached middle age but all that says is the best is yet to come. All of our mistakes have been made and learned from and now we have the wisdom and freedom to make the other half of our life really count."

I place my elbows on the table and lean in closer, gazing into his eyes dreamily. "I couldn't have put it better myself."

He does the same and leans closer to me and holds my attention with those captivating eyes. "So, what do you say to letting go of your doubts and inhibitions and seeing where this thing will go?"

I can't break away from that lustful stare and feel the desire bubbling up inside. I smile as sexily as I think appropriate for a public place and say huskily, "I think we should get the bill, don't you?"

Well, Edward can certainly move fast when he wants to because it must be within ten minutes that we are hurtling towards the apartment like a couple of giggling teenagers. Thank goodness for the Dutch courage inside me because now all I have bouncing around inside me is excitement and desperation to do what I've been fantasising about for months. Finally!

The next morning

I wake up in the absolutely huge bed of the master bedroom next to the man who showed me what I've been missing out on. Wow and double wow. Last night was incredible. It was everything I thought it would be with whipped cream on. Not that there was actually any whipped cream involved, mores the pity, but it was 10/10, 100% and A***.

Thank goodness for inhibitions and wise friends to turn to in our times of crisis. To think I nearly bottled out of the most amazing night of my life.

Edward stirs beside me but then settles back to sleep. I take a moment to admire the man himself. A little shiver runs through me as I remember being in his arms. It didn't feel odd or embarrassing. If anything, it felt the most natural thing in the world and as if I had come home at last. I don't even feel embarrassed to be next to him naked and needy. I am now Brandy the girl who lives life in the fast lane and seizes every opportunity. I love my new life which makes my decision even harder because it's not just about what I want. I will need to think this one through carefully because I'm not about to let this gorgeous man slip away anytime soon.

As I am now wide awake, I decide to spend a penny. Thinking it best to carry out that particular task in my own room, I grab his t-shirt from the nearby chair and head outside. I feel amazing. I feel confident and sexy and as if I can do anything I want. Edward has given me a new lease of life and now everything makes sense. I understand my mother's need to travel and crave excitement. I am like her more than I thought and surely if I'm happy, my children will be too. Yes, this is my future. I'm certain of it now.

I manage to make it to my room in time but just as I'm about to head back to wrap my body around

Edward's the skypy noise stops me in my tracks. I quickly answer it hoping it's my mother or one of the children but am astonished to see Robert looking at me anxiously from the other side. He looks worried and immediately the hairs stand up on the back of my neck. "What is it, Robert? Are the kids ok?"

He looks concerned. "They are fine. It's not them I'm worried about."

I sit on the bed and look at him with confusion. "What is it then?"

He peers even closer to the camera and says softly, "It's you, Amanda."

I look at him in shock. "Me? Why on earth are you worried about me?"

He looks at me like a social worker or something. "Saskia and Ryan are concerned about you. It would appear that every time they call, you are in bed and looking terrible."

Ok, way to make a girl feel good about herself.

He carries on. "It got me thinking and I'm sorry, Amanda."

I shake my head. "For what?"

He smiles gently. "I never thought about how hard all of this would be on you. I mean, I know it wasn't your choice for our marriage to end and yet here we are, enjoying my wedding without you. You must have found it hard all week watching the man you love marry another with your children by their side. Let me assure you that I've got this. You will always be my first love and hold that special place in my heart but you know we needed to move on. You will soon forget me and meet someone else when your heart has mended. Don't shut yourself away crying for what we had, go out and embrace life and do what makes you happy. You are a beautiful woman, Amanda and will make a deserving man very happy one day."

He smiles at me in such a condescending way that I want to punch the screen. Is this really what they think? That I have spent the week pining away in a strange bed in the Lake District for the man who abandoned me and his children for someone else. For the man who used to think he was being generous when he picked me daffodils from the park and gave them to me as a gesture of affection. For the man who did absolutely nothing in the way of housework and cooking and never changed a nappy once. For the man who went out with his friends every Friday night while I stayed in and did the ironing. Not forgetting the man who whined and complained that I didn't dress myself up like a hooker for the weekly sex sacrifice just to shut him up while I planned the next week's menu.

I look at him in total shock as he looks at me with sympathy. Then his eyes narrow and that condescending look is replaced by one of shock as he splutters, "Who the hell is that?"

I look around and burst out laughing as Edward stands behind me dressed only in a towel and looking every inch the love god, he is. Unshaven, tousled hair with a smattering of dark hair on a very muscly chest. His biceps are impressive and he nods to Robert as he places his arm around my shoulder and sits down beside me. He says good-naturedly, "Hi, you must be Robert. It's good to meet you. I'm Edward, Amanda's boyfriend. Sorry for the lack of clothing, it's early morning in Florida, we must look a mess."

I stifle a giggle as Robert's face turns to thunder and his eyes narrow along with his lips. He says tightly, "Oh I see. Well, you certainly kept that quiet didn't you,

Amanda? I wasn't aware you had a boyfriend and took off as soon as you could, lying to your children at the same time. I'll leave it up to you and your conscience to set them straight. Anyway, I can see I was concerned about nothing, so I'll leave you, um... to it then."

He snaps the screen shut and Edward laughs softly. "I'm sorry, Amanda, I couldn't help myself. That guy is a serious idiot and needed telling. I'm sorry if I've put you in an awkward position with your family."

Laughing, I turn to him and hug him as tightly as my thin arms will allow. "Thank you, Edward. You just made my day. I knew you were the man for me and it's not just the supply of Krispy Kreme's and coffee that decided it for me."

Laughing, he pulls me on top of him and smiles sexily. "Let me show you another reason why I'm the man for you."

I laugh softly, "Yes, maybe I do need to be convinced just a little more."

CHAPTER 37

Snapping my case closed, I look around the little apartment that has come to mean so much to me. This is where it all began. Where *we* began. Edward and me and our new life together. It feels like forever ago and yet has only been seven days. I am a very different person leaving than the one who arrived.

Our last days were spent abandoning the reason we were here in the first place. Instead, we spent our days and nights getting to know one another. I'm not convinced it would make a great travel article but we don't care. All that matters is that we found each other and now real life is about to intervene and bring us crashing back to reality. I can't deny the fact I'm nervous to face my family. I'll have to come clean to my children and face their accusatory faces as they hear about the reality of my week away. I must be the worst mother in motherdom because I have lied to them. I will never live this down but I'm past caring. Edward and I are now a couple and will face this together.

I take one last look around the apartment as I wait

for Edward to return. He's loading up the car and appears as down as me about leaving.

As I head towards the balcony for one last photo of the amazing view the iPad rings again. My heart lurches as I wonder what it will be today. I answer it and see Saskia staring at me with excitement.

"We're coming home tomorrow, mum. I actually can't wait to see you."

I smile, feeling an instant love hit as I look at my baby's face. "Me too. I've missed you and Ryan. Where is he by the way?"

She rolls her eyes. "He hit on some woman at a bar last night and never came home. Apparently, he needs to shake the fixation he has for Brandy who has totally blanked his message. He's out of control, mum. I mean, if it was me going out spending the night with random men I've picked up in the bar, I would be called all sorts. Dad just shook his head and said boys will be boys. What's that all about? Can you imagine if I did the same? He wouldn't be so understanding then, would he? It's not fair the double standards placed on a young life. I say equality for every female and we should all be encouraged to do what the hell we like."

Pushing aside the anxiety I'm now feeling for my son I think about her words. I'll remind her of those when all of this blows up in my face.

I smile and feel the happiness flood through me at the thought I'll be back with them tomorrow. I've missed them so much and it felt really strange that they weren't with me.

Suddenly, her eyes narrow and she leans closer to the screen. "Are you wearing my new top?"

Looking down I can see I've been caught red-handed

and smile guiltily. "Sorry, I didn't have anything else. I hope you don't mind."

She looks about to blow a fuse when we hear a loud, "Amanda, honey. I can't believe you're leaving me today."

Looking up my world starts to unravel before me as Chase rushes in and puts his arm firmly around my shoulder while planting a massive kiss on my cheek. Time stands still as Saskia looks at us with complete and utter shock. Chase looks at the screen and beams, "Hey, you must be Saskia. Your mom's told me heaps about you. She didn't tell me you were so hot though."

Saskia opens her mouth but no words come out for once in her life. Chase doesn't appear to notice anything strange and carries on. "You know, your mom's the best. Her ball skills are awesome and she's been the best partner a guy could wish for all week. She certainly knows how to party and I can't believe she's leaving me already."

Saskia looks at us incredulously as Nate joins in the fun. He lands on my other side and puts his arm around my other shoulder and grins at her. "Hey, honey. You should have been here. We've had the coolest week. You're so lucky to have such a fun mom. Chase is totally bummed she's leaving. Hey, you should come with her next time. We could show you around college and you can see how we party over here."

Saskia suddenly finds her voice and smiles. "That sounds great. I would really like that because I am actually thinking of applying for college over there, anyway."

The guys cheer and Chase grins at me. "Then you will have to come with her. It will be like old times."

I look at the three of them beaming with excitement and feel as if I'm living in a parallel universe. Saskia appears to have forgotten anything other than her own desires which helps a little. But I know my daughter and I have some serious explaining to do.

I stare at her guiltily and say softly, "Listen, I'll explain everything tomorrow. Have a safe journey and please WhatsApp me when Ryan shows up. I won't rest until I know he's safe."

She looks confused as I say brightly, "Anyway, sorry I must go. See you tomorrow, love you."

I snap the case closed and push the impending confrontation to the back of my mind. I will have 8 hours to worry about my homecoming. First, I need to thank the guys for making this such a trip to remember.

We swap numbers and WhatsApp details and I promise to keep in touch and then they leave. I'm sorry to see them go and hope we'll meet up again one day.

Edward heads back as they are leaving and says his goodbyes and then it's just the two of us.

We look at each other and share a look of resignation. Edward comes across and takes my hand and leads me onto the balcony where we stand hand in hand looking out over the picture-perfect view. He says softly. "I'll miss this place."

I sigh. "Me too. Everything's perfect here. *We* are perfect here. Despite the shaky start this is where I found you and the thought of returning home is both exciting and worrying at the same time. What if this cosy bubble bursts?"

He puts his arm around my shoulders and pulls me close. "This is just the beginning, Amanda. The start of many such trips and the start of a new life for both of us."

He turns to face me and I see a little spark of fear in his eyes as he says hesitantly, "That is if you still want to."

Smiling, I wrap my arms around him and hold him

close saying with determination, "That's the only thing I'm 100% sure about. I know I have some explaining to do but I'll get over that. We can make this work if we want it enough."

Edward pulls back and kisses me lightly on the lips, whispering. "I want this more than anything. Thank you for being the best travel companion a man and twitter could ask for."

Laughing, I shake my head and grin. "Well, my mother came good in the end, didn't she? Now I just need to get home and sort my family out and then we can start planning our next secret adventure."

Edward grins and kisses me long and hard to seal the deal. This may be the ending of the beginning but we have so much to look forward to as we start the most exciting half of our lives.

CHAPTER 38

I am so nervous and can't keep still. We got home yesterday around lunchtime and I brought more than just an incredible suntan home with me. Edward came back, and we spent the night at my house because neither of us wanted to say goodbye.

But that's just what's happened because Edward left this morning to return home and leave me to square things with my family. He won't be gone long, though, because we have plans to meet up for dinner the day after tomorrow after I've spent some time with my children.

I'm nervous because any minute now they will return, driven by my ex-husband and will be demanding answers.

As I wait, I think about the last couple of days. The flight home was very different to the one out and Edward and I sat in business class as a couple. A sort of meeting in the middle. Not first class or economy but slap bang in the middle. It felt good to have someone to share everything with and use as a pillow on the long night flight home. I feel so comfortable with Edward. Has it really just been a few days since we pushed aside our instant dislike and fell in love so deeply?

I was a bit nervous bringing him home and wondered if I would feel differently when the familiar came back to claim me. But he looked as if he belonged in my home and far from it seeming strange, it now just feels empty now he's gone.

I see the car making its way steadily up the cul-de-sac and feel the nerves bubbling up. This is it. Explanation time, which will probably involve lots of tears and tantrums and heated exchanges. Despite it all, I can't wait to see my children. One week seems like months and I wonder if they've changed at all.

With a pang, I realise this is now the norm for Robert. He doesn't see them for weeks on end and I wonder how he copes with it. I know I'd hate it. They are part of me and it feels as if that part's missing when they are gone. I hope that Robert managed to spend quality time with them this week because it won't be long before they make their own lives and just visit occasionally.

The car door slams and I steel myself for the conversation I'm about to have. Flinging the door open, the tears threaten to blind me as I see my two gorgeous children exiting the car with uncharacteristic haste. Saskia reaches me first and to my surprise drops her bags – as usual – and clings to me like she did as a child. She says in a strangely emotional voice, "I missed you so much, mum."

I hold her tightly and feel my heart constrict. She missed me too. I can't believe it. Saskia never shows me this much affection. She must have hated every minute of her trip away.

She lets me go as Ryan takes her place and even

though he doesn't cling to me like a life belt, he does kiss me on the cheek and hold me tightly, whispering, "Good to see you, mum."

Ok, now I'm in shock. Who are these people? Has it really been that long?

Saskia appears super excited and grabs hold of my hand as they pull me inside. Robert follows looking a little cold but I don't care about that. If he didn't like the fact I had a man in my room, he shouldn't have left it in the first place.

Saskia looks around her and sighs with relief. "Thank god I'm home. It feels like forever and France is not England you know. It was ok I guess, but this is where I belong."

Robert looks a little miffed and says, "You seemed to like it at the time."

Saskia throws him one of her withering looks and shakes her head. "It was ok for you. You were doing everything you wanted to. Well, I'm sorry dad but trawling around battlefields and museums is not for the young. We get all our information from YouTube and the Internet these days and if I want to know what happened in the war, I can watch a film about it on Netflix."

I stifle a grin. Some things never change. I'm not sure trying to broaden Saskia's mind can be achieved in the space of one week but at least he tried. I smile at them all and say brightly, "Who wants a cup of tea?"

To my complete and utter surprise, Saskia says softly, "I'll make it, mum."

I think I'm in shock as she heads off and Ryan grins at me. "She missed you, we both did. It's good to be home, mum."

Tears bubble up behind my eyes as I look at my son and see the little boy looking back at me who used to think I was the most important thing in his life. He smiles which lights up his face and I see something there that wasn't there before. He looks happy and I hope it's because he spent a great bonding week with his father who set him back on the right path. He picks up his bag and smiles. "I'll just unpack and then I'll probably arrange to meet up with Mungo."

He turns to Robert. "Thanks, dad."

Then he heads upstairs leaving me in a total state of shock. Did he really just take his own bag upstairs?

Robert looks at me and nods stiffly. "So, you're back then."

I stifle the flash of irritation that threatens to ruin what is turning out to be an amazing homecoming and just smile.

"Yes, we got back yesterday."

He raises his eyes. "Yes, of course, you're a *'we'* now aren't you?"

Saskia chooses that moment to enter the room balancing a tray that seems alien in her hands. She looks at me with a hard look.

"Yes, mum. I think you have some explaining to do. Great tan by the way. You look ten years younger."

I sit down quickly on the settee feeling the shock hit me again. Whoever this Saskia is that's walked back in, is far better than the one who left. She sits next to me and hands me the first mug of tea that she's made for me in months and says excitedly, "Come on, spill everything."

Robert sits opposite and as if by magic Ryan also appears back in the room and looks at me with interest. So, I tell them my story and watch the disbelief grow on their faces with every word spoken.

By the time I've finished Saskia looks confused. "But

how do you know Brandy's boyfriend? You haven't mentioned her in any of this."

I feel myself turning red as I come clean about my alter ego. "I'm sorry, guys. I decided that I needed to learn more about your world and downloaded Instagram. I wanted to connect with you both without you knowing it was me, so I invented Brandy. Chase was just a friend I made on the first day there and when you told me that Ryan was stalking Brandy, I used him to put him off."

Ryan has turned quite pale and looks extremely disturbed. Saskia, however, looks as if all her Christmases have come at once. "So, you mean he isn't going out with a super blogger and you have his digital details. Oh my God, mum, you're a legend. I can't believe it. This is the stuff of dreams. I could apply for their college and we could become a super couple. He could show me around and fall in love with my accent. You hear it all the time. So, what is it, are you a super blogger now? I told you things had changed. Oh, my god, this is so cool. I can't wait to tell the others in my social circle. My mums a blogger like Zoella and our lives are about to explode."

Her eyes gleam as she starts making plans. "Well, first things first, we need a PO box. It's the law and I can't wait to activate it. Just think, Chloe Smith doesn't have a PO box. She'll be so jealous."

Robert looks at her with irritation. "Saskia, there's more to life than just a PO box. I think you should be concentrating on passing your GCSEs because no college will take you without them."

She rolls her eyes in true teenager fashion and looks at him as if he's from the dark ages. "Well, obviously. Honestly, dad, you really should drag yourself into this century. It's all very well living in the war but those men fought for the freedom we now enjoy. It would be disrespectful to their memory if I didn't live my life to the full you know."

Robert looks at her speechless for once and I stifle a grin. He never did understand her and I can see some things haven't changed.

She looks at me with interest. "So, what about you, mum? What happens next?"

I feel my heart thumping and take a deep breath. "Well, I'm not sure you know this but I have something to tell you."

Ryan and Saskia share a look and Robert adopts that stern look of a man who has never done anything wrong in his life. Certainly not one that abandoned his family for a new life without a thought for the one he left behind. I say nervously, "I kind of met someone, and he is now my boyfriend."

Ryan looks at me with surprise and Saskia smiles and says softly, "I'm happy for you, mum."

What?! I look at her in total surprise. She raises her eyes. "What? It's good you have a friend. Now I won't worry about you when I head off to college to be with Chase and Ryan joins the army."

Ok, rewind a minute. What???

I look at Ryan in shock as he says angrily, "Thanks, Saskia. You could have let me tell them."

Robert looks at me and the look on his face says this is as much of a surprise to him as it is to me.

I say weakly. "Since when?"

Ryan shrugs. "I've been thinking about it for some time. There was a guy who came to the school in careers week and I sort of got interested then. I've been to their offices in town a few times and found out a bit more about it. Mungo and me are joining up as soon as the exams are over. We want to join the navy because they do really cool things like in Top Gun."

I am actually speechless. Robert is looking so proud and I know it's because of his love of fighting and guns and things. However, I am devastated. He can't go to war and put himself in danger. He's my baby and should stay with me and become a solicitor or something safe and secure.

He looks at me anxiously. "I'm sorry, mum, but it's what I want. The recruitment officer said I could take you down there and he would explain everything. I don't need your permission because I'm 18 but I do want your blessing."

I feel empty, upset and so scared it hurts. But as I look at my son, I feel more than those things. I feel so proud of him. He is taking charge of his life and doing something he's interested in. My baby boy has become a man and who wouldn't feel proud about that?

Robert walks over to him and hugs him hard. "I'm proud of you, son. If I can help in any way, just say the word."

Seeing the two of them together like that brings a tear to my eye. Despite everything, we have made something amazing here in this room. Robert and I have raised two fantastic children who are turning out to be responsible adults. Saskia has dreams that include bettering herself even if they are a little misguided. I'm under no illusions that the thought of a hot guy is central to her new plans. Ryan looks happy and excited for once in his life and I feel the pride surge through me. Standing up, I move across and pull him in for a hug. I manage to choke out the words. "I'm so proud of you, Ryan. Of course, I'll support you. It won't stop me worrying about you though, you will always be my baby boy."

Saskia makes that gagging sound and Robert laughs. And so, this is it. In this room, at this moment, all our lives change. Our past counts for everything now because it's what brought us all to this point. We are a family and always will be. We may all be heading our separate ways but we will always have a place to return to. Wherever we end up, we will always have each other.

CHAPTER 39

It feels strange returning to work after what was only a week away yet feels like a lifetime. I feel a little nervous as I'm not sure how I'll feel. Edward and I discussed me working for him and it all sounds amazing but it may put a strain on our relationship. It's so early into it that I'm not sure if I can give up my career just yet. What if things don't work out? What if I'm left loveless and jobless? Things are moving on so quickly now; I should at least keep something familiar in my life.

However, my heart sinks as soon as I walk through those familiar doors. It seems a world away from what I now want. Do I really want to carry on making ends meet here, instead of living the dream with Edward travelling from one fantastic experience to another?

The first person I see is the checkout manager, Susan.

She smiles and says happily, "Thank goodness you're back. I'm so short staffed and don't suppose you could spare a few hours overtime today."

Shaking my head, I look at her apologetically. "Sorry, I have plans later. Maybe another time."

She shakes her head. "Never mind, it was a bit short notice. Anyway, how was your holiday, you look amazing?"

I can't stop the smile from breaking out on my face as I remember what happened last week.

"Let's just say it was life-changing, Susan."

She looks interested, but we are interrupted by the sight of Veg man wheeling a trolley nearby. I look at him with interest but that's all. There is no longer that same lurching feeling I used to get when I saw him. My heart isn't fluttering and I'm not watching his every move. If anything, he seems pretty ordinary now and way too young for me. He has nothing of Edward's rugged good looks and pure sexiness radiating off him like sonic waves. Veg man, dare I say it, looks boring in comparison.

Susan leans in and whispers, "Hold on to your heart, Amanda, that magnificent man is on the market again."

I look at her with interest. "Why, what happened?"

She whispers, "Emily was transferred to Kingston and almost immediately fell in love with the click and collect manager. Harry, was left high and dry and is now the focus of just about every woman that still has her natural urges in the place."

I look at him and feel a bit sorry for Veg man. I know more than most what it's like to lose someone to another and even though it's obvious he won't be alone for long; it still must have hurt.

Susan looks excited. "Maybe you will start shadowing him in produce when you start the management training programme next week. Who knows, you could be the next power couple of the superstore?"

Rolling my eyes, I shake my head. "Not me, Susan. I have my own plans and they don't concern Harry."

She looks surprised as she directs me to my register. As I sit behind the familiar station, I look around me and sigh. How is it that I've changed so quickly in such a short time? I always knew I wanted more from life but even I never knew there was really any other opportunity out there for me. Now, however, everything has changed and I'm at a crossroads, uncertain of the way forward.

I sit pondering my problem for a couple of hours before I notice a pack of Edam cheese travelling towards me, closely followed by a pack of Krispy Kreme doughnuts. My heart beats a little faster as I raise my eyes and stare into the extremely amused ones of Edward.

I look at him in complete surprise as he leans forward and whispers, "I can't do this without my partner in crime. I need you to agree to pack your bags and be my companion in every way. What do you say, Amanda, will you let me show you the world?"

I hold my breath along with the rest of the line it would seem. Edward is looking at me with such love and hope and something else. He is looking at me as if I am the most important person in the world and who on earth could refuse that? I stand up and nod, "Only if you let me take the photographs sometimes."

He grins and his eyes sparkle as he looks around and whispers, "Am I allowed to kiss one of the staff in this place."

I laugh. "Only if it's me."

Then he reaches across and pulls my face to his and kisses me so deeply that cheering breaks out all around us. As soon as he stops, he pulls away and grins happily.

"There's no going back now. We have witnesses and now you're mine."

I roll my eyes, "Actually, I think you'll find it's the other way around. Now you're mine and all that goes with me. Speaking of which, do you want to come and meet the rest of them later for tea?"

He nods and smiles happily. "I'll be around after work."

He pays the bill and as he walks away, I shout after him, "Don't forget the doughnuts."

CHAPTER 40

*E*dward arrives, as discussed, after work and I feel quite nervous about how this will go. What if the kids hate him? They may resent another man in their life taking their mother's attention from them. Remembering back to the conversations they had about Lucy, I'm not expecting miracles but a girl – sorry – woman, can hope at least.

Saskia watches me pacing around the front room and rolls her eyes. "Oh, for goodness sake, mum, relax will you. I'm sure he'll be fine. Hopefully he's not a weirdo or something and anyone that blogs for a living must be cool."

I smile nervously. "He is but it matters to me what you think of him. Anyway, where's Ryan he should be home by now?"

Saskia shakes her head. "He got off with Claire Musgrave last night at Mungo's party. He's hanging around at hers this afternoon."

Once again, I worry about my son. He's out of

control and no girl appears safe from his advances around here.

Suddenly, I see Edward's car pulling up outside and feel the excitement mixing with the nerves as I watch him head towards the front door. Wow, he looks super sexy in his suit, in fact, I want to rip it off him the moment he steps foot through the door. However, in the name of not shocking my daughter and remembering my role as a mother, I push down my lust and fling the door open and smile.

"You made it. Come in and meet Saskia."

He smiles reassuringly and follows me in as I chat incessantly to mask the nerves I'm feeling. Saskia looks up and smiles. "Hey, you must be Edward. I'm Saskia and I must say I'm so impressed with your career choice. I've got so many questions to ask you, as quite honestly, Edward it's a route I've considered taking for quite a few months now."

This time I roll my eyes as Edward is pulled down next to my daughter and immediately interrogated.

Leaving them to it, I head off to make the tea and within about 10 minutes the door opens and I hear Ryan call out, "Mum can Claire stay for tea?"

I think I stop in my tracks. Claire?? Ryan has brought a girl home at exactly the same time that I have brought a boy/man home. Who'd have seen that one coming?

Remembering my manners, I head out and smile at the nervous looking teenager lurking behind Ryan. "Of course, I'm pleased to meet you, Claire."

She smiles shyly and says 'hi' in a whisper as Ryan says airily, "We'll be in my room until tea."

I look at him in shock and suddenly have to deal with an unexpected crisis on top of the one I'm already dealing with. Images of his new-found love of man whoring spring to mind and I shake my head quickly. "Actually, could you meet Edward first? He's inside with Saskia and I'd love you to say hi."

Ryan looks a little put out but does as I say and heads to the front room. I almost consider locking them in so I can keep my *mother knows best* eyes on them. It comes to something when you don't trust your own son with a young girl's morality under your own roof. Maybe the army is the best place for him after all.

I introduce him to Edward and to my relief they sit down opposite him and listen to Saskia grilling him about the travel business. Ryan, to my delight, seems interested as Edward tells them about a safari he went on last year where a tiger jumped on their jeep.

I leave them to it and head back to the kitchen. Well, that went as well as could be expected. The kids seem to like him and haven't embarrassed me yet, so that's something I suppose.

As I carry on with my culinary preparations, I hear a sharp knock on the door and wonder who on earth could be calling now. It had better not be those Jehovah's witnesses that were around here the other week leaflet dropping. I felt sorry for them and offered them a cup of tea, ok it was because one of them was super fit but even so, it did set me on edge a little. He turned out to have one of those eyes that look the other way and I kept on looking around to see who he was talking to.

Before I can get to the door, I hear shrieking and the loud voice of my mother booming out. "Saskia, darling, you've grown even more. Slow down young lady, I can't keep up with you."

The relief hits me like a tidal wave. Thank god, she's safely home.

I rush out and stop dead in my tracks – she's not alone.

She sees me and a huge smile breaks out across her face as she says loudly, "Darling, you look amazing. That holiday obviously suited you. I told you travel broadens the mind. Anyway, speaking of which I want to introduce you to my husband, Cyril."

I look in shock at the very small man holding onto my mother's hand. He looks to be in his seventies and has a ruddy complexion that I'm sure is the result of his sea shenanigans. He positively beams at me and booms, "You must be Amanda. I can see the similarities to your beautiful mother."

I just stare at him in shock along with my children. My mother laughs.

"Crack open the bubbly, darling because I have had quite the trip."

Suddenly, she spies Edward and does a double take. "Who's this gorgeous man, Amanda?"

Edward looks at me with amusement and then stands and offers her his hand. "I'm pleased to meet you, I'm Edward, Amanda's boyfriend."

My mother looks as if she's about to cheer loudly and the relief in her face makes me slightly annoyed. Surely, I'm not that bad. She grabs his hand and then pulls him in for a hug. "Welcome to the family, Edward. I want to hear every minute of your time together."

Edward looks at me and raises his eyes as I blush and laugh nervously. "Don't be ridiculous, mum. If anyone has any explaining to do it's you. You go incommunicado for a whole week and don't even check your phone. I was having an emergency which then turned into an even bigger one worrying about you. And what's all this about a wedding? You had better start speaking and fast."

My mother pulls her new husband into the room and sits down beside him, holding his hand tightly.

"Well, we met the Jolly Rogers in a restaurant one night and struck up quite the friendship. They invited us to set sail with them around the island and I must say, we had quite the party, didn't we?"

He laughs loudly and booms, "Your mother is quite the party animal, Amanda. We had one wild time."

The children look slightly disturbed and Edward grins at me, obviously enjoying this whole experience.

My mother continues. "Well, the time just flew past. I couldn't inform you of my new plans because my phone ended up falling out of my bag when we stepped on board. It's probably on the ocean floor as we speak."

Saskia and Claire gasp with horror and Ryan shakes his head.

Thinking about it, I wonder how my mother coped with that. She's just like the kids, constantly glued to her phone at all times. She shrugs, "It didn't matter. I was having far too much fun to think about life outside the here and now."

I feel strangely annoyed that she wasn't in the least bit worried about her only daughter abroad with a stranger and she laughs as she sees my expression.

"Lighten up, darling. You're a grown woman now as am I. Anyway, when we returned, Cyril pleaded with me to stay. The other Jolly Rogers were also leaving and he would be all alone. So, I agreed to be his ship's mate which kind of led to other things."

Ryan and Saskia now look decidedly nauseous and Edward laughs softly as I stutter, "Enough detail already. Where did you get married?"

Cyril takes her hand and smiles sweetly at my mother as she looks at him fondly. "We found a little chapel up the coast and pleaded with the chaplain to marry us. It was so romantic and quite like Mamma Mia actually. So, now we are husband and wife and setting off for a life lived disgracefully."

I look at her with surprise. "What do you mean?"

She smiles happily. "We are going on a trip around the world and will start the planning immediately."

I sit down heavily and look at them in shock. "How will you afford that on your widow's pension?"

Cyril chips in. "Your mother needn't worry about that, I have enough money for the both of us. We will travel first-class and stay in the most luxurious hotels. This is one honeymoon that will last as long as we do."

Saskia looks majorly impressed and Ryan looks interested. I'm actually speechless and just let it all go on around me. My mother talks about their plans excitedly all evening and the children listen with a great deal of interest. Then it's their turn as they fill their grandmother in on their own plans.

Then we tell her all about our own plans to travel and she looks at me with such pride it almost hurts.

"Good for you, darling. I'm so happy, I always knew you had it in you. Just trust in yourself and follow your dreams and look where they take you. I'm proud of you all."

As we all sit talking long into the night, it strikes me how much our lives have changed so quickly. It just goes to show that if you believe in the unattainable and seize the moment, dreams can come true and you can have it all. It's true, we only have one life and that doesn't stop when you're married or a parent. Even my mother in her seventies has no fear and forges on regardless. She's a great role model and the most fantastic person I know. She has never settled for what life tells her she should be doing and has always gone out and lived her life as if it's her last day. She embraces change and has no fear. There's always more and we shouldn't be afraid to seek it out.

Then I look at Edward and as our eyes meet, I feel complete. Whatever else I want from life it's with him right beside me. Never stop dreaming and never stop trying. You never know what it will throw at you so don't waste a minute of it. I hope when I'm in my 90s I'm with Edward travelling the world and looking for new experiences. I hope that my children are happy and fulfilled and live a long and healthy life with the people they love. That's all it's really about anyway. Isn't it?

~

Thank you for reading More From Life. If you enjoyed it you may like Escape to Happy Ever After.

Escape to Happy Ever After where all your happy endings are guaranteed.

When Susie Mahoney was gifted a break to Happy Ever After she couldn't pack her bags quickly enough, she had to do something to break the run of bad luck she was experiencing.

She was fast approaching the age where all her friends had settled down and found their 'one' and she was running out of options.

Happy Ever After, as it turns out, is a sweet little bed & breakfast on the Dorset coast and as soon as she sets eyes on the little cottage nestling in a valley before a sparkling sea, she falls in love.

Surely this is the perfect place to set her life back on track and consider her options. Long walks in the fresh air to concentrate her mind. Hearty meals to raise her energy levels and cosy evenings in the local pub beside a flickering fire curled up with a good book. Perfect.

However, what she didn't realise was the invitation was for two and her 'plus one' was already unpacked and making himself at home. There is also a Fossil club convention in town meaning every room on the Jurassic coast is occupied and she has to spend the next week with a stranger.

Freddie Carlton receives an invitation to escape to Happy Ever After and was particularly interested in the 'happy ending' it promised. Having had a disastrous run of bad luck with women he was prepared to try anything.

He wasn't prepared to discover that his 'one' had already been chosen for him and was seriously annoying. A woman who arrived with more baggage than an Airbus and was in no mood to share.

Will Happy Ever After work its magic and give them both the happy ending they deserve, or will fate continue to throw obstacles in their path and turn their bad start into a very complicated ending?

Escape to Happy Ever After.

BEFORE YOU GO

Thank you for reading More from Life.

If you liked it, I would love if you could leave me a review, as I must do all my own advertising.

This is the best way to encourage new readers and I appreciate every review I can get. Please also recommend it to your friends as word of mouth is the best form of advertising. It won't take longer than two minutes of your time, as you only need write one sentence if you want to.

♥

Have you checked out my website? Subscribe to keep updated with any offers or new releases.

When you visit my website, you may be surprised because I don't just write Romantic comedy.

I also write under the pen names M J Hardy & Harper Adams. I send out a monthly newsletter with details of all my releases and any special offers but aside from that you don't hear from me very often.

I do however love to give you something in return for your interest which ranges from free printables to bonus content. If you like social media please follow me on mine where I am a lot more active and will always answer you if you reach out to me.

Why not take a look and see for yourself and read Lily's Lockdown, a little scene I wrote to remember the madness when the world stopped and took a deep breath?

sjcrabb.com

Lily's Lockdown

(Just scroll to the bottom of the page and click the link to read for free.)

STAY IN TOUCH

You can also follow me on the Social media below. Just click on them and follow me.

Facebook

Instagram

Twitter

Website

Bookbub

Amazon

ALSO BY S J CRABB

The Diary of Madison Brown

My Perfect Life at Cornish Cottage

My Christmas Boyfriend

Jetsetters

More from Life

A Special Kind of Advent

Fooling in love

Will You

Holly Island

Aunt Daisy's Letter

The Wedding at the Castle of Dreams

My Christmas Romance

Escape to Happy Ever After

sjcrabb.com

Printed in Great Britain
by Amazon